遠野物語

The Legends
of Tono

遠野物語

The Legends
of Tono

100th Anniversary Edition

KUNIO YANAGITA
柳田國男

TRANSLATED BY RONALD A. MORSE

LEXINGTON BOOKS

A division of
ROWMAN & LITTLEFIELD PUBLISHERS, INC.
Lanham • Boulder • New York • Toronto • Plymouth, UK

LEXINGTON BOOKS

A division of Rowman & Littlefield Publishers, Inc.
A wholly owned subsidary of The Rowman & Littlefield Publishing Group, Inc.
4501 Forbes Boulevard, Suite 200
Lanham, MD 20706

Estover Road
Plymouth PL6 7PY
United Kingdom

British Library Cataloguing in Publication Information Available

Library of Congress Cataloging-in-Publication Data

Yanagita, Kunio, 1875–1962.
  [Tono monogatari. English]
  The legends of Tono / translated by Ronald A. Morse. — 100th anniversary ed.
    p. cm.
  Includes index.

  ISBN-13: 978-0-7391-2767-4 (cloth : alk. paper)
  ISBN-13: 978-0-7391-3024-7 (e-book)

  1. Folklore—Japan—Tono-shi Region. 2. Tono-shi Region (Japan)—Social life and
customs. I. Title.
  GR341.T63Y3613 2008
  398.20952—dc22   2008020776

Printed in the United States of America

♾™ The paper used in this publication meets the minimum requirements of
American National Standard for Information Sciences—Permanence of Paper for
Printed Library Materials, ANSI/NISO Z39.48–1992.

This translation is for Jackie and Randy Morse.

CONTENTS

PREFACE TO THE 100TH ANNIVERSARY EDITION

This new edition of *The Legends of Tono* (*Tono monogatari* in Japanese) was prepared in celebration of the one hundredth anniversary of the original Japanese-language publication in 1910. The preface and introduction to this new edition were updated, and a guide to works related to Kunio Yanagita was added in the back of the book.

The reader can approach this volume in one of several ways. If interested in the original work, the legends and literature, it is best to go directly to the original 1910 translated text of *Tono monogatari* and read that. If the reader would like some background on Kunio Yanagita and Tono before reading the main body of *The Legends of Tono*, the introductory material provided in the front section of the book is an excellent source. And if research and what other scholars have written on Kunio Yanagita intrigues, the reader should go to the guide on English-language materials provided in the back of the book.

When Kunio Yanagita (1875–1962) published *Tono monogatari* in 1910, he had no idea that within several decades his work would become a Japanese literary and folklore classic. There are many reasons for the continued popularity of *The Legends of Tono*: Yanagita's ability to create a literary image of the Tono area, the psychological depth and directness of the stories, Yanagita's terse literary and poetic style, and the originality of the perspective on local spiritual life presented in the collection.

Tono monogatari, given its position in the documenting of the Japanese oral folk tradition, is also often compared to *Kinder-und Haus-Märchen* (*Grimms' Fairy Tales*, 1812), the Germanic folktale collection by Jacob and Wilhelm Grimm. Indeed, it is often mentioned that Yanagita was probably motivated to write *Tono monogatari* after having read *Grimms' Fairy Tales*.

Yanagita considered writing a literary work like *The Legends of Tono* for some time before 1910, and it was only after his discussions with people from Tono that he discovered the setting and stories to realize his dream. Another reason *Tono monogatari* remains popular in Japan and abroad is because it is seen as the starting point for Yanagita's development of the modern discipline of Japanese cultural and folklore studies. Having said that, A. W. Sadler finds both the literary and folklore aspects of the work lacking. He sees the images that Yanagita captures of a harsh and brutish social order as only anticipating a great literary work. And he finds none of the classification and trappings of classic folklore research in *The Legends of Tono*.

Either way, scholars interested in Yanagita's study of Japanese folk traditions view *Tono monogatari* as a critical work in Yanagita's transition from the literary phase of his career to his more academic interest in defining the science of Japanese folklore studies. This is discussed in greater detail in the introduction that follows.

In translating *Tono monogatari*, I have tried to preserve the flavor of the original document as much as possible. The objective has been to convey Yanagita's gift for careful observation and a crisp classical Japanese literary style of expression. There were no maps and few illustrations in the 1910 edition of *Tono monogatari*. I have included some of each of these where I felt that they would be useful to readers less familiar with the Tono area and its culture. Some explanatory notes have also been added where they seemed helpful.

Although there are many Japanese-language editions of *Tono monogatari* currently available, when I originally translated this work in 1975 I relied on the text in a Japanese literary collection, *Nihon Kindai Bungaku Taikei* (vol. 45, *Yanagita Kunioshu*, Kadokawa Shoten, 1973, 257–312).

For readers of Japanese, there is now one volume that annotates nearly every detail found in the original *Tono monogatari*. This 406-page compendium of information is the result of nearly a decade of research by the Tono Jomin Daigaku (Tono Citizens' College) group under the direction of Kunio Yanagita researcher, Professor Soichiro Goto. See *Chushaku Tono monogatari* (*Explanatory Notes and Commentary on The Legends of Tono*), Chikuma Shobo, 1997. This work lists the large number of dictionaries, guidebooks, and scholarly studies that have been published in Japanese about *Tono monogatari*.

Translators often have to make difficult and sometimes unpopular choices. Japanese who have checked and double-checked my translation for accuracy have generally praised the work. Some American scholars, however, have questioned my English translation of the book's title as *The Legends of Tono*. It was Richard M. Dorson (1916–1981), the eminent American folklorist who had actually studied with Yanagita in Japan and who wrote the foreword to this translation, who insisted that I translate the Japanese word *monogatari* into English as "legends," not "tales." He maintained that legends, as distinct from tales, were local and had a distinct regional personality. For more on this, see Richard Dorson's foreword to the original 1975 edition.

Those questioning my translation have maintained that my English translation of the title should have been *The Tales of Tono*, because some stories that could be considered tales are included in the text. Others, who see *Tono monogatari* as having a unified literary purpose, maintain that the translation should have been *Tale of Tono*, as in the case of the *Tale of Genji*. For readers interested in these and other issues surrounding Yanagita's career, I have included a guide to various reading sources.

This volume was the first translation of *Tono monogatari* to be published in English or any foreign language, and it was only possible with the help of many friends. A leader in Japanese local history studies, Daikichi Irokawa, who was visiting Princeton University in the early 1970s, first pointed out to me the importance of *Tono monogatari* for understanding Japanese grassroots culture. Back in the early 1970s, when I was doing research on Kunio Yanagita in Tokyo, Yasuo Kijima, my neighbor, was of invaluable assistance in explaining Tono dialects and Japanese phrases I had difficulty translating. Kijima, a poet and writer in his own right, subsequently published two of his own books on Yanagita's literary career. Kijima also took responsibility for designing and publishing the first version of my translation in 1975. Since then, we have been close friends and traveled to Tono together on several occasions. Another neighbor in Tokyo in the early 1970s, Francie Dawson, convinced me that any attempt at a literal translation would not be adequate. I followed her advice as well.

Jackie Morse, my wife since 1961 and companion on trips to Tono, patiently, but not always willingly, typed (and retyped) the original translated text. Professor Kensuke Tamai, at Princeton University, and California-based folklore expert Fanny Hagin Mayer, a translator and expert on Japanese folk literature, each checked my translation for accuracy and made many useful suggestions. Coworkers in the Department of Defense where I was working in 1974, Harry G. Rosenbluh and Marcia F. Wackerhagen, assisted in editing the final draft. Professor Marius B. Jansen (1922–2000) of Princeton University, my Ph.D. advisor and a brilliant scholar in the field of Japanese studies, was instrumental in getting the Japan Foundation to publish the first edition of my translation in 1975. When the first printing of five thousand copies was sold out in 1990 (the eightieth anniversary of the original publication), the Tono City UNESCO Association reissued two thousand copies of my translation using different artwork. Now that these books are also sold out, it seemed appropriate to prepare this new and updated edition to celebrate the one hundredth anniversary of the publication of the original work.

Over the years, many people in Tono City have been extremely helpful to me. In particular, I would like to thank Hisao Ishida, of the Tono City Cultural Affairs and Exchange Department, for his encouragement and kindness. Tono City's mayor, Toshiaki Honda, has always been receptive to new ideas and is a great supporter of international understanding of Tono and Japan. Tono City generously provided the photographs used in this book.

This one-hundredth-anniversary edition would also not have been possible without the cooperation of many other people. Mrs. Fumiko Yanagita, Kunio Yanagita's daughter-in-law, kindly provided Japanese copyright permission for Yanagita's work. She has a residence in Tono City and is active in cultural projects there. The Japan Foundation also generously gave their permission for the 1975 English translation text to be reissued. Beverly Stevenson and Mary Schramski read the final manuscript and provided valuable advice. Osamu Atsumi was a constant source of encouragement. Patrick Dillon at Lexington Books, who was responsible for this publication project, was also extremely helpful.

Japanese names are in the Western order—that is, personal name followed by family name.

Ronald A. Morse
Las Vegas, Nevada

FOREWORD
TO THE 1975 EDITION

Richard M. Dorson (1916–1981)

The name of Kunio Yanagita is well known throughout Japan. Any time I mentioned it during my Fulbright year in that country (1956–1957), my Japanese acquaintances responded with instant recognition, whether or not they shared my professional commitment to folklore. My own interest in Yanagita-*sensei* derived from his fathering of folklore studies in his country. Through good fortune my residence that year in Tokyo was situated in Seijo-machi, the other side of the *densha* (train tracks) from the Japanese Folklore Institute he had established next door to his home, and I spent much of the winter in the institute (in the nick of time, because it closed in the spring) for lack of financial support.

On several occasions I visited Professor Yanagita, then in his eighty-first year, and talked with him through an interpreter. My impressions remain of a Buddha-like figure, benign, serene, composed, but commanding and receiving deference, a large, well-formed, handsome man, full-featured and smooth-faced. He entered readily into my plan for a volume of monographic essays to be written by leading Japanese folklorists, all his protégés, and translated into English in order to introduce the work of his school to scholars abroad. To that volume, published as *Studies in Japanese Folklore*, he contributed a gracious interview on opportunities for folklore research in Japan, calling attention to the "enormous possibilities for folklore study" in the traditional culture of his homeland.[1] In particular, he stressed the opportunity to reconstruct the ancient religious faith, pretty much erased by Christianity in the Western world, but discoverable and decipherable in the pre-Buddhist mountain and ancestor worship still practiced in Japanese villages. This was the target and the method of his school: historical reconstruction of the old animistic religious system, the *minkan shinko*, from which external accretions imposed by outside cultures must be peeled away.

The output of folklore publications by Yanagita staggers the imagination: close to one hundred books and one thousand articles. In the comprehensive bibliography of Rene Sieffert, *Etudes d'ethnographie japonaise*, titles by Yanagita appear under every category of ethnographic and folkloric research.[2] Sieffert wrote, *Sa biographie devient une immense bibliographie*. True, Yanagita did not personally write and assemble all these dictionaries, monographs, collections, and field manuals, but he directed and supervised those that he did not actually produce, and he wrote so much of his own that he was obliged to publish under pseudonyms. Yet only a handful of Yanagita's monumental output has been translated.

All the more welcome, therefore, is the present translation of his first folklore work, the *Tono monogatari* of 1910, which opened his eyes and ears to the living abundance of the Japanese oral tradition and caught the fancy of his countrymen. In presenting the legendary tales told by Kizen (Kyoseki) Sasaki, an educated member of a peasant Tono household, Yanagita had tapped the most vigorous stream of Japanese storytelling, the *densetsu*, or local legend, more intimately bound with village daily life and thought than the fictional *mukashibanashi*, or fairy tale. *Tono monogatari* takes its place with the *Kinder-und Haus-Märchen* of the brothers Grimm as a landmark collection in the history of folklore studies opening the way for subsequent collecting forays that have now become commonplace endeavors.

But as the Grimms operated under what we now regard as a misconception of the nature of oral narrative, so did Yanagita. These pioneer collectors judged oral tales by the yardsticks of written literature and felt a responsibility to "improve" the rough and unpolished specimens of the peasant's delivery. Sasaki was not a good storyteller, wrote Yanagita. Today, we would disagree. The sheer volume of Sasaki's legend repertoire assures that quantitatively he was indeed a good storyteller, with over one hundred legendary traditions in his head. Today, folklorists recognize that oral style differs greatly from literary style and needs to be considered in terms of its own aesthetic, on the basis of faithfully reproduced verbal texts. The legend is by its nature more conversational and seemingly fragmentary than the structured fairy tale. In the two examples of fairy tales included in *The Legends of Tono*, we see that Sasaki could master fictional storytelling as well.

While dozens of *densetsu* collections have followed and emulated *The Legends of Tono*, compiled by individuals or by local groups, Yanagita's first book remains the only one to capture a whole body of village legendry from a single teller. Sasaki reflects all the pervasive themes characteristic of *densetsu*, as illustrated in my own sampler from the village collections, *Folk Legends of Japan*. Tono has the *kami* (spirits) who guard home, hearth, and privy; goblin creatures like *kappa* and *tengu*; rich men, or *choja*, who encounter fortune and misfortune; evil foxes with powers of transformation; warriors and fools who make magic; and spirits of the dead and of the mountains, who blend in with *kami*. The old animistic folk beliefs envelop the scene, and demons lurk everywhere, in monkeys and wolves, in rocks and ponds, and in the forms of mysterious strangers encountered beyond the village boundary. Some of the Tono legends closely parallel examples in *Folk Legends of Japan*, as in the wrestler who discovers his opponent has been a transformed fox that made off with his dinner, or the spirit of the drowned woman heard weaving at the bottom of the pool, or the *kappa* dragged by the horse from the pond into the stable.[3]

There is a hint by Sasaki of the gruesome legend of *Ubasute-yama*, in his reference to the custom of sending old people over sixty to an appointed place to die.[4] Yanagita's longtime fascination with mountain folk religion can be appreciated from *The Legends of Tono*, with their ascription of spirit beings to the mountains. All these incidents, seemingly discrete and sometimes trivial, form parts of an organic whole, the supernatural life of Tono, freighted with deities and demons who continually interact with mortals.

What is of special interest in the present collection, and which distinguishes it from the later village legend-books, is the personal and firsthand character of many of the *densetsu*. Folklorists separate the legend, which is a collective property of a group of people with some common associations, from the memorate, a remarkable and extraordinary experience told in the first person. The memorate often grows into legend, but in so doing it loses its quality of immediacy. In *The Legends of Tono*, memorates predominate. Sasaki tells what he has seen and felt, or what his family, friends, and neighbors have witnessed. The details of killing the sister of Yanosuke the flute player (story numbers 9–11) by her mad son, even to his placing a commode for her inside the house, bespeak the closest association with the persons involved, presumably with Yanosuke himself, who though deep in the mountains heard his sister's dying scream. Her final wish, that she die without feeling hate or vengeance toward her son, brings the grim episode directly within the sphere of *minkan shinko* (folk religion), which holds that the spirit of a person dying with a hateful heart will continue to haunt its enemy and must be placated by a shrine and offerings. In *The Legends of Tono*, Sasaki offers the vision of a typical Japanese villager who grows up in a world fraught with dangers from invisible forces and malevolent creatures shuttling between the human and animal kingdoms.

In making *The Legends of Tono* available in English translation Ronald Morse, the perceptive biographer of Yanagita-*sensei*, has placed Asian and folklore scholars in his debt. It deserves a wide attentive audience outside its own country to match the readership it has rightfully earned at home.

NOTES

1. *Studies in Japanese Folklore*, ed. Richard M. Dorson (Bloomington: Indiana University Press, 1963; repr. Port Washington, New York: Kennikat Press, 1973), 51–53.

2. *Bulletin de la Maison Franco-Japonaise* (Tokyo, 1952), Nouvelle Scrie, II, 9–110.

3. *The Legends of Tono* no. 94, and Richard M. Dorson, *Folk Legends of Japan* (Tokyo/Rutland, Vt.: Charles E. Tuttle Co., 1962), 129–32, "The Fox Wrestler"; *Tono* no. 54, and *Folk Legends*, 110–11, "The Weaving Sound in the Water"; *Tono* no. 58, and *Folk Legends*, 61, "The Kappa of Koda Pond."

4. *Tono*, no. 111, and *Folk Legends*, 222–25, "The Mountain of Abandoned Old People."

INTRODUCTION

Ronald A. Morse

The Tono region, not far from the Pacific Ocean coast in Iwate Prefecture in northeastern Japan, provides the geographical setting for *The Legends of Tono*. The indigenous Ainu people, who were the earliest inhabitants of the area, gave Tono many of its place names. Tono, a rugged mountainous area with rice cultivation in the valleys and lowlands, was historically rich in gold and lacquer and was an excellent climate for raising horses. But life was not easy. The stories in *The Legends of Tono* (*Tono monogatari*) present the severe weather conditions, frequent crop failures, and limited arable land, all of which made making a living difficult for the local inhabitants.

The local ruling warlord family, the Nambu, lived in the Iwate area since the eleventh century but only became politically influential in the seventeenth century. It was in the nineteenth century that mining activities became more important and new areas were opened to rice cultivation. By the time Kunio Yanagita visited Tono for the first time in August 1909, railroads had extended to nearby Hanamaki City, and the

Kunio Yanagita in 1949

forests of Tono were being used to make railroad ties and produce wooden matches.

Kunio Yanagita was moved to write of *The Legends of Tono* for a variety of reasons. As a young man, he was an avid reader of Chinese ghost stories, classical Japanese literature, and had been exposed to *Grimms' Fairy Tales*. He also traveled extensively throughout Japan when he was with the Ministry of Agriculture and Commerce. In 1908, after he became the secretary to the Imperial Household Agency, he was also given the task of reorganizing the government Cabinet Library. It was probably in the Cabinet Library that he discovered sixteenth- and seventeenth-century local government accounts of the Tono area that he used as reference when drafting his text for *Tono monogatari*.

But the catalyst for Yanagita to put pen to paper came from a casual encounter with a young man from Tono in 1908. Yanagita, then active in Tokyo literary circles, was introduced to the young writer Kizen (Kyoseki) Sasaki (1886–1933), a native of Tono. He listened with fascination to Sasaki's narrations of legends and stories from Tono. Sasaki is specifically mentioned in the preface of *The Legend of Tono* and in legends 17, 22, and 59.

Fascinated by the deep cultural content of the stories told by Sasaki, Yanagita decided to visit Tono from August 23–26, 1909, to verify firsthand his impressions of Tono. He stayed at the Taka-zen Inn, which is now a museum in Tono City, and rented a horse to travel around the area. It was on August 25 that Yanagita visited the Tenjin area shrine, which provided the dramatic festival scene presented in the introduction to *The Legends of Tono*. In Tono, Yanagita also met with the local scholar and historian Kanori Ino (1867–1925) to learn more about the region. Yanagita visited Tono again in 1920 and 1926.

Yanagita always wanted to write a novel, and *The Legends of Tono* came

Kizen Sasaki

about as close to being a novel as Yanagita ever got. Yanagita's final edits to the text were, unlike his later works, done more with an eye to impressing his literary friends in Tokyo than to faithfully documenting the Tono districts folk traditions. The writing of *Tono monogatari*, however, demonstrates what might be called Yanagita's folklore methodology—listen carefully (the oral tradition), go and see the location for oneself (visual and tangible cultural observation), verify any facts with local experts, write up the results so that the average person can appreciate and understand the subject, and, as was the case with *The Legends of Tono*, add some literary flair (to capture the local sensibility and spirit). In this way, Yanagita was able to portray the enduring, some would say the more culturally universal, qualities of Tono peasant life.

For Yanagita, the geography and history of Tono were an ideal backdrop for exploring the feelings, psychology, and beliefs of the people of the Tono region. The legends in *Tono monogatari*, as narrated by Yanagita, portray two worlds: the observed world, made up of physical images of mountains, rivers, houses, and place names; and the concealed world, where spirits and gods come and go with ease. Aditionally, the world of Japanese folk religion (temples,

A Tono City Street Around 1909

shrines, festivals, and a multitude of deities) connects the world of everyday life to a higher spiritual order, and Tono becomes an ecosystem traversed by a vast array of natural and supernatural beings.

The Legends of Tono opens (in the introduction) and closes (with the song of the Dance of the Deer) with the images and sounds of a local festival. Central to Tono festivals is the sword-wielding warrior dancing opposite the blue and white decorated deer figure with flute players performing a local story-song in the background. This dance is called *shishi odori*, which literally means "lion dance." The lion, or *shishi*, can be a dog or a deer, but in Tono it means "deer." The *shishi*, or deer, often a deity or an agent of a deity, has magical powers and the ability to repel evil spirits. In Tono each village has its own deer costume design, head dress decorations, and words for the "Dance of the Deer" song.

The deer is central to Tono folk culture because it moves freely between two worlds: the world of ordinary people and the powerful forces of nature. It is both a deity and the animal that damages the village rice crops. The deer symbolizes the spirits in the mountain in tension with the hunters and farmers in the valleys. It represents the indigenous Japanese folk religion of the mountain people in tension with the Buddhist religion introduced into the lowlands from

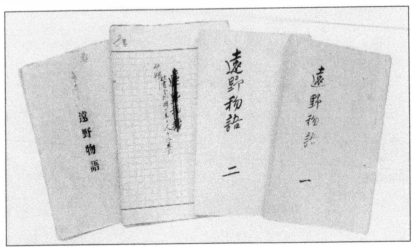

Original Drafts and First Edition of *Tono monogatari*

India and China. And the deer, in the folk psychology, represents the forces that humans must deal with as part of life.

For Yanagita, the local village Shinto shrine was the center of peasant religious life. Festivals, usually associated with harvests in August and September, were the seasonal expression of the psychocultural dimensions of folk faith. The village shrine was where history and religion, community and ancestors, the living and the departed spirits came together and gave meaning to life.

After completing his final editing of the work in June 1910, Yanagita paid a printer to publish 350 copies of *Tono monogatari*. Most of the copies of the book were given to family members and friends. Copy number one was given to Kizen Sasaki, in thanks for stimulating Yanagita's literary interest in Tono and its folk traditions. That copy of the book is now on display in the Tono City Museum. Also, all three of Yanagita's early drafts of the text with his editings are preserved in the Tono City Library. *Tono monogatari* was first commercially published in the 1920s.

Yanagita, then still active on the Tokyo literary scene, considered *Tono monogatari* a literary work, written more like a novel than as a contribution to Japanese folklore. Yanagita published a number of other nonliterary works around the same time—one book on hunting terms in southern Japan in 1909 and a study of small stone gods in 1910. Late in 1910, he also published a study on agricultural policy, in which he had a growing interest.

Only a few book reviews of *Tono monogatari* were published when it appeared and most of those by Yanagita's literary friends. Katai Tayama, a leader of the naturalist literary movement in Japan, wrote critically that "Yanagita's work has an impressionistic quality. . . . I find the work infused with an extravagance of affected rusticity. I remain unmoved."

In 1935, Kizen Sasaki added a separate appendix of 299 legends to the original *Tono monogatari*, but these legends lacked the literary qualities of Yanagita's earlier work.

In more recent times, *The Legends of Tono* has generated a broad spectrum of commentary. The late Bunzo Hashikawa, a professor at Meiji University, compared *The Legends of Tono* with the Chinese revolutionary writer Lu Xun's collection of essays from the 1920s and 1930s, *Old Tales Retold* (*Gu Shi Xin Bian*). *Old Tales Retold* is a volume of old Chinese fables rewritten from a modern critical perspective. Lu Xun (Zhou Shuren, 1881–1936) was a student in Japan between 1902 and 1909 and deeply involved in Japanese literary circles at the time.

The leftist writer Ryumei (Takaaki) Yoshimoto wrote a Freudian interpretation of *The Legends of Tono*, comparing it with the Japanese classic *Kojiki* (*The Record of Ancient Matters*, 680 AD) in his *Psychic World of Shared Fantasies* (1969). Yukio Mishima, the nationalist writer, wrote favorably about the eerie literary qualities of *The Legends of Tono*. (See the guide at the back of this book to find English translations of Mishima's comments.)

In 1976, a popular writer from the Tono region, Hisashi Inoue, poked fun at Yanagita's work in his *New Reading of the Tales of Tono* (*Shinsaku Tono monogatari*). Inoue wrote his stories about Tono with an earthy humor and more local color than Yanagita. This work has been translated by Christopher Robins.

The only full-length English-language academic study of *Tono monogatari* is a 2001 doctoral dissertation by Melek Ortabasi.

KUNIO YANAGITA

Kunio Yanagita (1875–1962) attended elite schools, had good political contacts through his brothers, served in government briefly, dabbled in literary circles, was a journalist for a short time, worked at the League of Nations, and then settled into a lifetime of studying Japanese rural agricultural life and folk history.

Kunio was born into the Matsuoka household. Following his graduation from Tokyo Imperial University in 1900, he was adopted into the influential Yanagita household and married a daughter of the Yanagita family. Handsome, well-educated, and now free of financial worry, Yanagita could do whatever he wished. He traveled widely throughout Japan and never became identified with any one political position or school of thought. He was a very private person, and the public statements he made were generally noncommittal. He encouraged other people in their studies but was not personally interested in developing a group of loyal followers who could continue his Folklore Institute or line of research.

Yanagita, like his father (a Shinto priest) and his brothers, was open-minded, but conservative and patriotic. As a bureaucrat, he couched his criticisms of the government in suggestion. He supported government efforts to strengthen Japan but was critical of the superficiality of many attempts at social reform. As a journalist, he recorded his times with a naturalness and sensitivity that has given his reporting an enduring quality.

As a youth, his reading of history and his interest in *kokugaku* (the National Learning School of Japanese cultural studies) shaped his interest in Japanese folk religion. Between 1900 and 1915, the writings of British folklore scholars provided a framework for his research. And his extensive travel and fieldwork throughout Japan contributed to the vast body of information that become the cornerstone of Yanagita's rural folklore studies.

Yanagita's college years coincided with a period of great literary excitement in Japan. The mood of the period was captured in Katai Tayama's *Tokyo no sanjunen* (*Thirty Years in Tokyo*, 1917):

> It was fascinating how the main streams of European literature entered Japan. Into the midst of the small peaceful world of 3,000 years of [Japanese] insularity, Bushido and Confucianism, Buddhism and superstition, *giri* (duty) and *ninjo* (human feeling), humiliating sacrifice and endurance, and compromise and social intercourse, came Nietzche's unsparing criticism, Ibsen's resistance, Tolstoy's ego, and Zola's dissection.

Among Japanese intellectuals there was a thirst for things foreign in the Meiji era. Hearing of a new foreign-language book or translation, Yanagita and his friends would rush off to the bookstore and then debate about what they learned late into the night. It was also during these years that Yanagita read *Grimms' Fairy Tales*. According to folktale translator Fanny Hagin Mayer, who studied with Yanagita in Tokyo, Yanagita had a good reading command of French and English and knew some German and Dutch.

Despite the trendiness of the times, Yanagita retained his restrained manner of literary expression. This was probably the result of his early training in poetry, especially the composition of *tanka* (short poems). Yasuo Kijima, a Japanese poet and biographer of Yanagita, maintains that Yanagita's poetry is filled with traditional images of the Japanese landscape, a device used to get at the spiritual, often dreary, world that extends behind mere surface appearances.

When Kizen (Kyoseki) Sasaki (1886–1933) first narrated the Tono tales to Yanagita, Yanagita immediately recognized their literary value. Sasaki, then an aspiring twenty-five-year-old writer, was introduced to Yanagita by the poet and writer Yoshu Mizuno in 1908. Mizuno and Yanagita belonged to the same literary club in Tokyo at the time. Sasaki's personal letters, writings, and book collection are now preserved in the Tono City library.

In composing *Tono monogatari*, Yanagita edited his draft three times, each time adding more geographical detail and sharper imagry. In his final edit, he also added about ten legends. By putting the narrative into the first person, he also enhanced the work's literary impact.

If there is a unifying theme to Yanagita's life work, it is the search for the elements of Japanese tradition that explain Japan's distinctive national character. In *Japanese History and Folklore*, Yanagita explained his folklore methodology in this way:

> There is no single unrecurring event in the history we seek to know. The life of the people in the past was a cumulative phenomenon that was renewed through the strength of the group. . . . We must look for multiple examples. If there are no old records, we must search among the facts that have survived into the present. By comparing these facts, it will be possible to establish a method that traces the evolution of change.

THE LEGENDS OF TONO

What makes these legends unique is the fact that the peasants are not the object of scorn and ridicule. Instead of the usual moralizing about what should be in life, the legends are filled with examples of discord, unfilial behavior, fraud, self-interest, protest, arrogance, and distrust. This cluster of seemingly negative, primary emotions is presented as a part of the human condition.

Evaluations of *Tono monogatari* have varied over the years. When the work first appeared, the novelist Toson Shimazaki commented that Yanagita was a gifted observer whose travel was a vital factor in his writing. Kyoka Izumi, who was acquainted with the northeastern region of Japan and himself a writer of ghost stories, found the legends fascinating. Katai Tayama labeled the work "an extravagance of affected rusticity." Shinobu Origuchi, a poet and folklorist, saw the ideas of *kami* (spirit or deity) and *yamabito* (mountain men) as central to Yanagita's concern but questioned whether this represented the whole of Japanese religion.

Tono monogatari, written as it was midway in Yanagita's life, is instructive of the direction of Yanagita's later interests. In this work, he was attempting to explore what he later defined as the essence of the Japanese national personality. In *Tono monogatari*, Yanagita used the tangible phenomena of buildings, food, religious objects, and annual observances in combination with the verbal devices of tales, dialects, ballads, and poetry to explore the mental and emotional makeup of the Tono residents.

Standing also as it does on the border between literature and history, *The Legends of Tono* has its own distinctive character. Some readers find the psychological implications of the legends to be of primary value. Others are moved by the combined sense of intimacy and awe that Japanese feel toward their deities. And there are those that find the fear of strangers and the pervasive sense of isolation or loneliness in Japanese culture.

Because of the city's rich folklore, Tono has become a popular tourist destination in the northeastern part of Japan. The Tono City library, built in 1986, has a wealth of local historical and folklore materials. A new crafts and hostel farming village was opened in 1996, and the attractive Aeria Hotel near the city library and museum provides a pleasant setting for conferences and Tono cultural events. Tono's city-wide festival is held every year from September 14 through 15.

This festival, which ends at Hachiman Shrine, consists of parades, archery contests, deer dancing, and community float competitions.

In 2007 an animated movie directed by Kenichi Hara, *Summer Days with the Kappa Coo* (*Kappa no Koo to Natsu Yasumi*), used Tono as a setting for a good part of the film. A *manga* (graphic novel) series by Kimi Takamuro titled *Tono e-monogatari* (*Tono Tales in Pictures*) was funded by a local resident, Seikan Kikuchi. Traditional chanters of local tales still perform on a daily basis in the city. The restored historical district near the museum has a gallery using a section from Yanagita's original home in Tokyo. Fumiko Yanagita, the daughter-in-law of Kunio Yanagita, has also established a Kunio Yanagita Folk Traditions Meeting House in Tono where meeting and seminars can be held. There is also the restored Takazen Inn where Yanagita stayed when he first came to Tono. Close by is the active Tono Monogatari Research Center, which conducts seminars and sponsors research projects related to *Tono monogatari* (www .tmkenkyu.com/). A vast array of *kappa* toys, folk legend CDs, and local foods of every kind are also now available throughout the city.

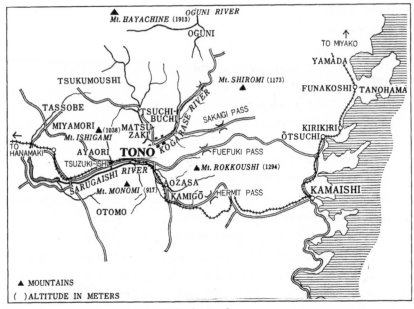

Map of Tono Locations Mentioned in the Book

It is personally gratifying to know that over the past thirty-five years my translation of *Tono monogatari* has allowed non-Japanese a glimpse into the world of Japanese folk customs and folk literature. I have also been fortunate in having the chance to visit Tono City several times over the years. I encourage the readers of this book to visit Tono and explore its rich traditions firsthand.

遠野物語

The Legends
of Tono

by

KUNIO YANAGITA
柳田國男

THIS BOOK IS FOR PEOPLE
LIVING IN FOREIGN COUNTRIES. *

Kunio Yanagita

* Yanagita elaborated on this statement in 1935, saying: "In 1910, when this book first appeared, an unusually large number of my friends were in Europe or were about to leave for Western countries. It was then, while thinking of sending them a copy, that I wrote this dedication."

PREFACE

All of the tales and legends recorded here were told to me by Kizen (Kyoseki) Sasaki who lives in Tono. I have been writing these stories down since February 1909 just as he told them to me during his many evening visits. Kizen is not a good storyteller, but he is honest and sincere. I have written the stories down as I understood them, without adding a word or phrase. I imagine there are hundreds of other legends in Tono similar to the ones written here, and I earnestly hope they too will be heard in the future. In the mountain villages of Japan, in areas yet deeper into the mountains than Tono, there must be countless other legends about people and spirits in the mountains. I wish these legends could also be heard, for they would not only make those of us who live in the lowlands shudder but would also provide a fresh start like *The Legends of Tono*.

I visited Tono during the latter part of August in 1909. Within forty kilometers from the town of Hanamaki there are only three towns; the rest of the area is green mountains and open fields. The houses here are far less scattered than those on the Ishikari plain on the northern island of Hokkaido. One reason for this might be that only a few people have settled there since roads first opened.

The old castle town of Tono is still flourishing. I rented a horse from the innkeeper and rode around to the nearby villages. The horse I rented had dark seaweed hanging over its sides and back to protect it from the numerous horseflies. The valley along the

Saru-ga-ishi River was fertile and well cultivated. There were more tombstones along the roadside than I had seen in other areas. Looking out from a high point, I could see that the rice plants planted earlier were just ripening and the late rice plants were in full bloom. The water had now been drained off the rice fields and out into the river. The shades of the rice plants changed with the plant variety. In places where three, four, or five fields had the same color of rice plants, it probably meant that they belonged to one household and probably had the same place name. The place name of any area smaller than a *koaza* was only known to the owner. The name could only be found in the old documents concerning land-sale transactions.

Tenjin Hill Shrine

I went across the valley of Tsukumoushi and from there Mt. Hayachine, which was off in a thin mist and appeared shaped as a pointed grass hat, or like the shape of the Japanese phonetic katakana alphabet letter *he*. Here in the shaded valley, the rice plants were late in ripening and were still quite green. Walking along the narrow path between the rice fields, a kind of bird that I did not recognize crossed over in front of me with her young. The young birds were black with white feathers mixed in. At first, I thought they were young hens, but when they hid themselves among the grasses in the ditch, I knew they had to be wild birds.

At Tenjin Hill (Sugawara Shrine), there was a festival, and the Dance of the Deer was being performed. A light cloud of dust rose from the hill, and bits of red could be seen against the green backdrop of the whole village. The dance in progress, which they called a lion dance, was actually the dance of the deer. Men wearing masks with deer horns attached to them danced along with five or six boys who were dressed as warriors waving swords. The pitch of the flutes being played was so high and the tone of the song so low that I could not understand what they were singing even though I was just off to the side. The sun sank lower and the wind began to blow; the voices of the drunkards calling out to others were lonely to hear. Girls were laughing and children were running about. I could not help but feel the loneliness of being just a traveler.

During the Buddhist Bon Festival,[1] it is the custom for families in which someone has recently died to hang out a red or white flag to welcome back the soul of the dead. Sitting on my horse in a mountain pass, I could point to some ten locations east and west where these flags were flying. Villagers were about to leave their lifelong homes, travelers drifted into the village, and a calm settled on the mountains of the souls; the dusk of twilight hovered over them all and then covered them up. In Tono there are eight locations with Kannon (the Buddhist Goddess of Mercy) temples. Each Kannon image is made from one tree. On feast days, numerous worshipers come to pray and lighted torches can be seen on the hillside. The sound of gongs can be heard in the brush, and at the fork in the road there are large straw figures used in the Rain and Wind Festival. The straw figures were on their backs like a tired people.[2] These impressions have stayed with me from my visit to Tono.

I think a book like *The Legends of Tono* goes against present-day literary fashions. No matter how easy the printing of this book might be, some people will maintain that it is harsh for me to publish it and attempt to force my limited tastes on others. Nevertheless, I would reply by asking the question: Is there anyone who, after hearing these stories and seeing Tono, would not want to tell others about it? No one that quiet or cautious can be found among my friends.

Quite contrary to the nine-hundred-year-old tales in *Konjaku monogatari* (*Tales of Long Ago*), the legends of Tono reveal facts that exist before our eyes. I cannot say that the legends from Tono are superior to those in the *Konjaku monogatari* in their sense of piety or sincerity. But in the sense that the legends from Tono have neither been heard by many nor recited nor written down to any degree, I believe the candid and innocent author of the *Konjaku monogatari* named Dainagon-dono would surely come to hear them.[3] Also, the tales of the *Otogi hyaku monogatari* written during the Edo period (1603–1868) have now lost their originality, and the author could not vouch for their accuracy.[4] It would be a shame if these older tales and stories were compared to those existing today. *The Legends of Tono* are present-day facts. This alone is their raison d'être.

Kizen Sasaki is now twenty-four or twenty-five years old, and I am only ten years older than him. During the present era with so many things for us to do, it is hard for us to appreciate the magnitude of things to accomplish. What defense could I make if I failed to use my strength to record these legends when I could? Some might reproach me for having ears too strained and eyes too big, like the eared owl of Mt. Myojin, but what can I say? I can say nothing, and I alone must accept the responsibility for this work.

Knowledgeable,
Yet pretending to be old,
Motionless and quiet,
Off in the forest, the owl
Is probably laughing.[5]

NOTES

1. This festival, a mixture of Buddhist and folk traditions, is observed between July 13 and 16. During this time the souls of the dead are welcomed home. They visit at the family altar before being seen off again.

2. Storms are especially severe in this area around harvest time. The straw figures mentioned here are put up to protect the village from the wind and the rain. There are usually two straw figures, one male and one female. The figures are either placed at the outer border of the village or burned. This custom is also mentioned in legend 109.

3. Minamoto-no-Takakuni (1004–1077) is considered to have written the *Konjaku monogatari*. He was usually referred to as Uji Dainagon because he lived in the town of Uji and had the court rank of Dainagon.

4. The *Otogi hyaku monogatari* (1626) is a collection of Buddhist, Chinese, and Japanese tales.

5. This poem is probably referring to younger Kizen Sasaki (the owl) off in Tono (the forest).

LEGENDS OF TONO

1. The Tono region, which comprises the western half of what is now called Kamihei in the old province of Rikuchu (now Iwate Prefecture), is a plain surrounded by mountains. Under the Meiji administrative structure, the area consisted of one city, Tono, and the ten villages of Tsuchibuchi, Tsukumoushi, Matsuzaki, Aozasa, Kamigo, Otomo, Ayaori, Masuzawa, Miyamori, and Tassobe. During the earlier Edo era, the region was called the district of Nishihei, and, during medieval and ancient times, the area was called Tono-ho. The town of Tono is now the administrative center of the district, but in earlier times it was a castle town for the ten-thousand-rice-bale-rich territory of the feudal lord named Nambu. The castle was called Yokota Castle.

Once you get off the train in the town of Hanamaki, you must cross the Kitakami River and go east along the valley of the Saru-ga-ishi River for some fifty kilometers in order to reach Tono. Tono is quite busy for such a remote town. It is said that in ancient times the whole region was a lake and it was only after the water drained off into the Saru-ga-ishi River that the villages developed. Because so many mountain streams feed into the Saru-ga-ishi River, people call it the river of seven *nai* and eight cliffs. The word *nai*, meaning "ravine" or "swamp," can be found in many of the place names in Oshu, the northeastern area of Japan.[1]

1. The *to* in the word *Tono* is the Ainu word for "lake." The word *nai* (swamp) is also an Ainu term. The Ainu are descendents from Japan's first culture in the Jomon Era (14,000–300 BC).

—∞—

2. The town of Tono is located where two rivers running north and south intersect. Formerly, farm products for sale were gathered from up to forty-five kilometers back into the seven valleys around Tono. On market days, as many as a thousand people and a thousand horses crowded into Tono. The highest mountain in the region is called Mt. Hayachine, and it is to the north of the Tsukumoushi valley. To the east of Tono stands Mt. Rokkoushi. Mt. Ishigami, lower than the two other mountains, is between the areas of Tsukumoushi and Tassobe.

A long time ago there was a female *kami* (god) who came to this plain with her three daughters, and they put up for the night at the location of Izu Gongen[1] Shrine, in present-day Rainai[2] village. Before going to sleep the mother *kami* told her daughters that she would give the best mountain to the one who had the finest dream. Deep into the night when a lotus flower floated down from heaven and came to rest on the bosom of the eldest sister, the youngest sister, who would wake up now and then, secretly took the flower and placed it on her bosom. Thus, the youngest sister got the best mountain, Mt. Hayachine. Her sisters got Mt. Rokkoushi and Mt. Ishigami. Each of the three young female *kami* took up residence on their own mountain, and even now they rule over these mountains. Women in Tono are told, even today, not to climb these mountains lest they arouse the jealousy of these *kami*.

1. *Gongen* refers to the incarnation of the Buddha in the form of a *kami*.
2. The words *Tassobe* and *Rainai* are Ainu terms. The *rai* of Rainai means "death" and *nai* means "swamp." This probably refers to the fact that at one time the water in the area was still and quiet.

—∞—

3. A *yamabito* (mountain man) is someone who lives deep in the mountains.[1] A man named Kahei Sasaki, who is now over seventy years old, still lives at Wano in the village of Tochinai.[2] When Kahei was young, he went back into the mountains to hunt and came across a beautiful woman seated on a small rock combing her long

black hair. Her face had a beautiful whiteness about it. Bold and fearless, he raised his gun, aimed, and brought her down with one shot. He ran up to where she was and found her to be rather tall. Her untied black hair was longer than she was tall. Thinking of it as evidence of his shooting skill, he cut off a lock of her hair, looped it up, and put it into his chest pocket. He headed home, but along the way he felt too sleepy to continue the long walk. So he stepped into the shade and dozed off for a while. While Kahei was still on the border between sleep and waking, a man, also quite tall, drew close to him, stuck his hand into Kahei's chest pocket, took the loop of black hair, and ran off. At that moment Kahei woke up and said, "That must have been a man who lives in the mountains."

1. Mountain men and gods are also mentioned in legends 89, 90, 91, 93, 107, and 108.
2. Kahei is also mentioned in legends 41, 60, 61, and 62.

—ᵐ—

4. In Yamaguchi village, a household head named Kichibei went to Mt. Nekkodachi to cut some bamboo grass. He wrapped the grass into bundles, put it on his back, and was about to stand up when the wind came rustling across the field of bamboo grass. He looked up and saw a woman with a baby on her back come out of the woods in the distance and walk across the bamboo grass toward him. She was fascinating, and, as in the previous story, she had long black hair trailing behind her. The straps that fastened the baby to her were made from wisteria vines. Her kimono was of the common striped cloth, and the lower part, which was worn out, was patched with a variety of leaves. Her feet did not seem to touch the ground. She approached unhesitatingly, passed indifferently before him, and went off into the distance. His illness, which began with the fright of that moment, continued for a long time. He recently died.

—ᵐ—

5. Since ancient times, there has been a mountain road called Fuefuki-toge (flute-blowing pass) going from the Tono district over to Tanohama and Kirikiri on the ocean coast. The pass is a shortcut from Yamaguchi village[1] to Rokkoushi, but in recent years people going over the pass have always met a mountain man or a mountain

woman on the way. Out of fear, people have come to use the pass less and less. Finally, a different road in the direction of Sakaigi-toge (boundary-tree pass), which has a stable for changing horses at Wayama, was opened. Now people use this new road even though it is over seven kilometers longer.

1. Yamaguchi (mountain entrance) village got its name from the fact that it is the starting point for climbing Mt. Rokkoushi.

—∞—

6. In the Tono district a wealthy farmer is still referred to as a *choja*. One day, the daughter of a *choja* at Nukanomae[1] in the village of Aozasa was suddenly kidnapped and hidden by someone. A number of years later, a hunter from the same village went into the mountains and came across a woman alone. Frightened, he was about to shoot her when she said:

"Aren't you my uncle? Don't shoot!"

Surprised, he looked more carefully and realized that she was the favorite daughter of the *choja*.

"What are you doing here?" he asked.

She replied, "I was brought here by someone, and I am his wife. I have had many children, but he eats them all. I am all alone now. I will spend the rest of my life here with him, but don't tell anyone about me. You are in danger now, so please leave at once."

It is said that he ran off without finding out where she was living.

1. Many stories mention heaps of rice bran found near village boundaries. Nukanomae refers to the village in front of *nukanomori* (rice-hull forest). *Nukanomori* is the same as the *nukanotsuka* (rice-bran mounds) found in various areas. There are many *nukanomori* and *nukanotsuka* in the Tono region. Rice-bran husks cover the rice grain. Rice is milled to remove the outer husks of the grain and then the inner-most husk. The inner husk (*nuka*) is rice bran, and it is used as oil and in pickling.

—∞—

7. The daughter of a peasant from Kamigo village went into the mountains to gather chestnuts one day and never returned. Her family, thinking she had died, conducted a funeral ceremony using the girl's pillow as a symbol for her. Two or three years passed. One day, a man from the village went hunting around the base of Mt. Goyo and unexpectedly came across the girl in a cave concealed

by large rocks. They were surprised to see each other, and when the man asked why she was living there, she replied, "I came to the mountain to gather nuts and was carried off by a dreadful man who brought me here. I have thought of escaping but haven't had a chance."

He asked, "What does this man look like?"

"To me, he looks like any ordinary person, but he is very tall, and the color of his eyes is threatening. I have had several children, but he says that the children don't resemble him and are not his. The children are perhaps eaten or killed, but in any case they are all taken off somewhere."

Again he asked, "Is the man really human like us?"

"His clothing and appearance are quite common. Only the color of his eyes is a little strange. Once or twice between market days four or five people just like him get together, talk about something, and then drift off.[1] Because he brings food and things from somewhere, he must go into town. He might even return while we are talking."

It is said the hunter was frightened and returned home. More than twenty years have passed since then.

1. If the Tono market was held six times a month, this would mean that there would be five days between markets.

—ɷ—

8. In many areas of Japan, women and children playing outside at dusk often disappear in mysterious ways. In a peasant household at Samuto in Matsuzaki village, a young girl disappeared, leaving her straw sandals under a pear tree. One day, thirty years later, when relatives and neighbors gathered at her house, the young girl reappeared, very old and haggard. When asked why she returned, she replied, "I just wanted to come back and see everyone. Now, I am off again. Farewell."

Again, she disappeared without leaving a trace. On that day the wind blew very hard. The people of Tono even now, on days when the wind roars, say that it is a day when the old woman of Samuto is likely to return.[1]

1. The term *kamikakushi*, which refers to this phenomenon of women and children disappearing, means "hidden by a *kami* (spirit)." This divine kidnapping is said to be done by *tengu* (long-nosed goblins), foxes, demons, and *kami* (gods). When someone is abducted, the villagers conduct a search while beating drums and calling out the person's name.

—ɷ—

9. An old man named Yanosuke Kikuchi led packhorses on the trail when he was young. He was a good flute player and would play during the night while leading the horses. One slightly cloudy moonlit night, when he was going with a group of friends over Sakaigi-toge (boundary-tree pass) on the way to the seashore, he took out his flute and played just as they were passing above a place called Oyachi.[1] Oyachi is in a deep valley thick with white birch trees. Below it there is a swamp with reeds growing. Just when he played the flute, someone at the bottom of the valley cried out in a loud voice, "Hey, you're good!" It is said that everyone in the group turned pale and ran off.

1. *Yachi* in the word *Oyachi* is an Ainu term for "swamp."

—ɷ—

10. Yanosuke went back into the mountains to gather mushrooms and built a small hut to stay in for the evening. Late at night, he heard a woman scream out in the distance, and his heart began to pound. Upon returning to his village, he found out that on the night he heard the scream, at the very same moment, his younger sister had been killed by her son.

—ɷ—

11. This younger sister lived with her only son. When relations between the daughter-in-law and mother-in-law got bad, the daughter- in-law would sometimes return to her parents' village and not come back. One day around noon, the daughter-in-law was in the house sleeping, when all of a sudden the son said: "I can't let my mother live any longer. I have to kill her today." He picked up a hand sickle used for cutting grass and began sharpening it. Seeing that he was serious, the mother began to reason with him and apologize, but he would not listen at all. The daughter-in-law woke up and pleaded with him tearfully, but he would not yield. Then,

seeing that his mother was about to try and flee, he locked the front and back doors. When she said that she had to go to the bathroom, he went outside and brought back a portable commode and said, "Do it in this." As evening approached, she realized the end was near and crouched by the side of the open hearth and just cried. The son took the well-sharpened sickle and approached her. First, he took aim at cutting her left shoulder, but the tip of the sickle hit the shelf above the hearth and did not cut her too deep. It was at that moment that Yanosuke, who was off deep in the mountains, heard the scream of the mother. The second blow struck the right shoulder, and as she held out against death, villagers arrived in surprise. They grabbed the son, called the police, and handed him over. This was still the time when the police carried nightsticks. When the mother saw her son arrested and being taken away, she, in the midst of a cascade of flowing blood, said: "I want to die without harboring any hatred. Please forgive my son Magoshiro." Everyone who heard her was deeply moved. While being taken away, Magoshiro started swinging the sickle again and chased the policemen. Because he was considered insane, he was released and went home. He is still living in the village.

—◆—

12. There is an old man named Otozo Nitta at Yamaguchi in Tsuchibuchi village. The villagers call him Oto-jii or "Old Oto." He is about ninety years old, sick and near death. Since he is old, he knows the old tales of the Tono district very well. He always says that he wants to tell the stories to someone so they will not be lost. But nobody wants to go near him to listen to the tales because he smells so bad. He is especially knowledgeable about the biographies of the lords of various smaller fortresses,[1] the rise and fall of households, a variety of traditional songs from the district, legends from deep in the mountains, and tales about people living back in the mountains. Unfortunately, Old Oto died early in the summer of 1909.

1. There were many fortresses in the area, and most were very small, often no larger than the compound of a well-to-do local lord. See legends 68, 111, and 112.

—◆—

13. This same old man lived alone in the mountains for several decades. He had come from a good family but squandered his inheritance away during his youth. He gave up all hopes for a worldly life, built himself a hut above a mountain pass, and made a living selling a sweet fermented rice drink to travelers. Packhorse drivers treated the old man like their father and were close to him. Whenever the old man had a little extra money, he would go down into town and drink. He wore a short coat made from red blanket material. He also wore a red hood. When drunk on his way home, he would dance in the middle of the town, but the policeman would not say anything. Having grown old and infirm, he returned to his native village and led a pitiful existence. All of his children had gone north to Hokkaido, and he was all alone.

—∞—

Family Celebrating Oshira-sama

14. In every village there is always one old household that worships the *kami* (spirit) Okunai-sama.[1] This old family is referred to as *daido*. The image of this *kami* is carved from mulberry wood and has a face drawn on it. A hole is punched in the middle of a square piece of cloth, and the cloth is pulled down over the image to make a garment. On the fifteenth day of the New Year, the immediate neighbors gather in the house to worship this *kami*.

There is also the *kami* Oshira-sama.[2] The image of this *kami* is made in the same way, and it is also worshiped when the villagers get together on the fifteenth day of the New Year. At this ceremony they sometimes put white powder on the face of the *kami* image.

There is always a tiny room about one by two meters in the house of the *daido*. Those who sleep in this room at night always experience something unusual. It's quite common, for example, for the pillow to get turned over somehow. Sometimes the sleeping person is grabbed and awakened or is shoved out of the room. No one is permitted to sleep quietly in this room.

1. Okunai-sama is the household deity that looks after the fate of the family. Other household deities watch over the hearth, the sleeping area, or the toilet.
2. Oshira-sama, an agricultural deity, is worshiped throughout northern Japan. See legend 69.

—ᨏ—

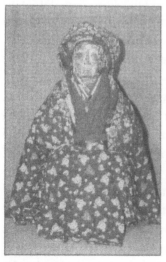

Okunai-sama

15. Celebrating Okunai-sama brings good fortune. At Kashiwazaki in Tsuchibuchi village there is a *choja* (wealthy farmer) named Abe. The villagers refer to his house as the house of rice fields. One year this household was short of hands to help with rice planting. The sky warned of rain the next day, and they were considering leaving some fields unplanted. Then all of a sudden a short boy came out of nowhere. He offered to help, so they let him work as he pleased. At lunchtime they called to him to come and eat, but they could not find him. Later, he reappeared and worked busily

the whole day in the fields. Thus, they finished all the planting on that day. They did not know where the boy had come from, but in the evening when they invited him to come and eat, he disappeared with the setting sun. When they returned home, they found the verandah covered with muddy little footprints that led into the parlor and up to the altar for the Okunai-sama. Thinking, "Well, what next!" they opened the door of the altar and found Okunai-sama covered from the waist down with mud from the fields.

—∞—

16. Many households worship the fertility god Konse-sama. The object worshiped for this *kami* is similar to that of Okoma-sama, which protects horses. There are also many Okoma-sama shrines in the villages. The object worshipped is a phallus made of stone or wood. Currently, this custom is practiced less and less.

—∞—

17. In older households there are quite a few families that have the spirit Zashikiwarashi (parlor child). Most of these spirits are twelve or thirteen years old. From time to time, they reveal themselves to people. At Iide in Tsuchibuchi village Kanjuro Imabuchi's daughter, who goes to a girls' high school, recently returned home

Konse-sama

for vacation. One day in a dark corridor, all of a sudden she bumped into Zashikiwarashi and was shocked. Zashikiwarashi was definitely a male child.

At Yamaguchi in the same village, the mother of Kizen Sasaki was sewing alone one day when she heard the sound of paper rustling in the next room. That room was only for the master of the house, but he was in Tokyo. Thinking it strange, she opened the door and looked in, but no one was there. Having sat down a short while, she now heard the sound of someone sniffing in the next room. She concluded that it must be Zashiki-warashi. It had been rumored for sometime that Zashikiwarashi resided in this house. A house that this *kami* (spirit) lives in is said to become rich and prestigious.

—𝕞—

18. Zashikiwarashi can also be a girl child. It has been known for some time that there were two of these girl *kami* in the house of Magozaemon Yamaguchi, also an old house in Yamaguchi. One year, a man from the same village, who was on his way back from town and near Tomeba Bridge, met two lovely girls whom he had never seen before. They were walking pensively toward him.

"Where did you come from?" he asked.

"We have come from Magozaemon's in Yamaguchi," they replied.

"Where are you headed now?" he asked.

"To a certain house in another village," was the reply. That house, in a somewhat distant village, is now a well-to-do farming family. Hearing this, the man conjectured that Magozaemon (since the girls were leaving) was headed for ruin. It was not too long after that when twenty or so people in the family died in one day from mushroom poisoning. Only one seven-year-old girl did not die. She merely grew old without having any children and recently died of an illness.

—𝕞—

19. Magozaemon was at home one day when he heard the servants discussing whether or not they should eat some unusual mushrooms that had grown up around a pear tree. Magozaemon, the master of his household, suggested that it would be best not to eat them. But one man servant said, "No matter what kind of mushrooms they are, if you put them into a water bucket and mix in hemp reeds there is no chance of getting poisoned." Everyone agreed with this, and they all ate the mushrooms. A seven-year-old girl was outside on this day absorbed in playing. The fact that she forgot to come home for lunch saved her.

After the sudden death of the master, and while everyone was still at a loss over what to do, family relatives from all around came and took all the household goods, even the soybean paste for cooking. The relatives said that they had loaned money to the master earlier or had some kind of agreement. This was a wealthy *choja* farm family, one of the first to establish the village, but in a single morning everything it had was gone.

—⚬—

20. Before this calamity there were signs of trouble. One day, when the men were taking out the hay with their pitchforks, they found a large snake. The master said not to kill the snake, but the servants

Family Around the Hearth

did not listen and beat it to death. After this, there were more snakes under the hay, and, when they wiggled out, the servants, partially for amusement, killed them all. Finally, needing a place to throw the snakes, they dug a hole, threw them in, and then made a dirt mound on top. There were so many snakes they filled several straw baskets.

—∞—

21. Magozaemon, mentioned above, was the scholar of the village. He had Japanese and Chinese books sent from the old capital of Kyoto, and he was usually absorbed in reading. He was somewhat eccentric. One day, he decided to find out how to get on good terms with a fox in order to make his house wealthy. First, he built an Inari (fox spirit) shrine in his garden. Then he went to Kyoto to obtain the highest official title for the fox deity. After that, every day without fail, he personally offered a piece of the fox's favorite fried soybean curd at the shrine and prayed. Gradually, the fox got used to him and did not run away when he approached. It is said that he could reach out and touch the fox on the head. The priest of the village's Yakushi (Buddha of Healing) Temple would joke, saying, "Nothing is offered to our Buddha, but it gives more benefits than Magozaemon's fox spirit."[1]

1. Four other legends are about foxes: 60, 94, 100, and 101.

—∞—

22. When the great-grandmother of Kizen Sasaki died of old age, the relatives assembled to put her into her coffin. Everyone slept together in the parlor that night. The daughter of the dead woman, who was insane and had been cut off from the family, was also in the group. Since it was the custom of the area to consider it bad luck to let the fire in the room die out during the period of mourning, the grandmother and the mother stayed up to watch the fire. The mother put the charcoal basket beside her and from time to time added it to the fire. Suddenly, hearing the sound of footsteps in the direction of the back door, she looked up and saw that it was the old woman who had died. She recognized how the bottom of the old woman's kimono, which dragged because she was bent over, was

pulled up as usual into a triangle and sewed in front. Other things were also the same, even the striped kimono cloth. Just as she said, "Oh!" the old woman passed by the hearth where the two women sat and brushed the charcoal basket with the bottom of her kimono. The round basket wobbled as it went around and around. The mother, who was a strong-nerved person, turned and watched where she went. Just as the old woman drew close to the parlor where the relatives were asleep, the shrill voice of the insane daughter screamed out, "Here comes granny!" The others were awakened, and it is said they were all shocked.[1]

1. Kunio Yanagita suggested this legend was like the play *The Intruder* (1890) by the Belgian dramatist Maurice Maeterlinck (1862–1949). Maeterlinck's play is set in a gloomy old chateau and centers around a blind man with unusual spiritual powers.

—∞—

23. On the eve of the fourteenth day after the death of the old woman mentioned above, close relatives gathered and recited Buddhist prayers late into the night. Just as they were about to return home, they noticed the old woman sitting on a rock near the entrance with her back to them. From the shape of her back, they knew it was the old woman who had died. Because so many people saw her, there was no doubt that it was her. No one could really understand to what she had such a deep earthly attachment.

—∞—

24. Older families in various villages are called *daido* because they migrated to the region from the southern province of Kai in the first year of the Daido Era (806 AD). The fact that Saka-no-Ue-no-Tamura-Maro (758–811) made his expedition to control the Tono region during the Daido Era and the story that the province of Kai was the main territory of the Nambu branch family seem to have gotten mixed up in the usage of the term *daido*.

—∞—

25. When the ancestors of the *daido* first arrived in the Tono area, it was on the last day of the year. They hastened to put pine tree branches on the house gate for the New Year. But they no sooner got

one side finished than it was already the first day of the New Year. Even today these old families, for good luck, leave one side of the New Year's entrance decorations lying on the ground. Then they put up the sacred rice straw rope that hangs across the two sides of the entrance.

—⚲—

26. The Abe family is an especially well-known farming household in Kashiwazaki. There was a very talented wood carver in the family generations ago. Many of the Shinto and Buddhist images in the Tono district were made by him.

—⚲—

27. The Hei River that begins on Mt. Hayachine flows northeast and empties into the ocean at Miyako City. The river basin is called the district of the Lower Hei. The previous head of the *Ike-no-hata* (beside the pond) family in Tono was on his way back from Miyako one day. Just as he was passing by the deep point of Haradai in the Hei River, a young woman appeared and handed him a letter. She told him that if he went to a swamp midway up Mt. Monomi, which is behind Tono, and clapped his hands, the person for whom the letter was intended would appear. He consented, but on the way he began to feel uneasy about the whole thing. Then he met a religious pilgrim who opened the letter and read it. The pilgrim said, "If you deliver this letter a great disaster will befall you. You should take a different letter." The pilgrim gave him a new letter.

When the man took the letter to the swamp and clapped his hands as he had been told to do, sure enough, a woman appeared and took the letter. As a token of her gratitude, she gave him a small stone grain-grinder. She told him that if he put a grain of rice in the grinder and turn it around, then gold would come out of the bottom. Thanks to the power of this precious object his family became very wealthy.

But his wife, a greedy person, tried to put a lot of rice into the grinder all at once. The grinder spun around of its own accord and fell into the water that the head of the house sprinkled on the grinder every morning as a way of saying thanks. The grinder disappeared. This small pool of water then became a pond, and it is still beside the house. They say that this is why the family is referred to as *Ike-no-hata.*

—⚬—

28. It was after the Nambu household had come to Tono that a certain hunter from Tsukumoushi village opened the first path up Mt. Hayachine. Up until that time, no one from the area had ever been up the mountain. The hunter, having cleared only half of the mountain path, was staying in a temporary hut he had built. One day while eating some rice cakes that he had toasted over the fire, someone passing by the hut stopped and peeked in. Looking carefully, the hunter saw that it was a large stranger with a shaved head like a Buddhist priest. The stranger entered the hut and gazed in wonder at the toasting rice cakes. Then, unable to resist, he reached out, took some cakes and ate them. The hunter, quite frightened, picked up some cakes himself and gave them to the man. The man was pleased and ate them. When all the cakes were eaten, the stranger left.

Thinking the man would come back again the next day, the hunter placed some white stones that resembled the rice cakes along with the cakes over the fire. The rocks became quite hot.

The stranger came back as expected and ate the rice cakes as he had done the previous day. Then he put a hot stone into his mouth thinking it was a cake. He charged out of the hut in shock and disappeared. It is said that the hunter later found the man dead at the bottom of the valley.

—⚬—

29. Mt. Keito is a steep peak in front of Mt. Hayachine. The people in the village at the base of the peak refer to the mountain as Mae-Yakushi. Fearful of long-nosed goblins (*tengu*) that live on the mountain, even those who climb Mt. Hayachine will not climb Mt. Keito. The head of the Haneto household in Yamaguchi was an intimate friend of Kizen Sasaki's grandfather. He was an eccentric fellow, who in his youth would do such things as cut grass with an

axe or turn up the ground with his sickle. He was also known for his rowdy behavior.

One day he made a bet and climbed Mae-Yakushi all alone. Upon returning, he told the story of how there was a huge rock on the top of the mountain with three giant men sitting on it. In front of them there were piles of gold and silver. Seeing him approaching they got angry, and the glare in their eyes was frightening. When he said that he had lost his way while climbing Mt. Hayachine, they said, "If so, we should see you off," and they led him down to a spot near the foot of the mountain. They told him to shut his eyes. When he opened his eyes the *ijin*[1] had disappeared.

1. *Ijin* has several meanings, including "ghosts," "goblins," "mountain men," "foreigners," or "strangers."

---

30. A man from Oguni village went to gather some bamboo on Mt. Hayachine one day. Amidst the thick, short bamboo plants he found a large man sleeping all alone. The man had taken off his huge meter-long bamboo sandals and was lying on his back snoring loudly.

---

31. In Tono, each year larger numbers of peasant children are kidnapped by *ijin*. Most are girls.

---

32. There is a swamp back in the mountainous area of Senba-ga-take (peak of a thousand nights). The valley there is dismal and smells of death, and few who enter these mountains ever come out. Once there was a hunter named Hayato. His children and grandchildren are still alive. He saw a white deer, followed it, and spent a thousand nights in the valley. From this came the name of the mountain.[1] This white deer was shot but ran away to the next mountain where it broke a leg. This mountain is called Mt. Katawa (lame mountain). The deer then returned to the former mountain, where it died. This spot is called Shisuke (dead person), and the Shisuke Gongen worships the white deer.[2]

1. White animals are ghosts or messengers for deities. See legend 61.

2. Kunio Yanagita suggested this tale was reminiscent of the stories in the Japanese *Fudoki*. In 713, an imperial edict ordered the various regions to compile descriptions of local history and customs. These reports are known as the *Fudoki*. The *Hitachi*, *Harima*, *Izumo*, *Bungo*, and *Hizen* area *Fudoki* remain today.

—ᴍ—

33. If you spend a night in the mountains of Shiromi, you would see that there is a dim light late at night. People who have gone there to gather mushrooms in the autumn and stay overnight in the mountains have seen this light. The crash of a big tree falling or the voice of someone singing can also be heard in the valley.

It is hard to measure the size of these mountains. In May, when people go to collect grass reeds, seen from afar, the mountains looks like piles of blooming paulownia flowers. It is as if the mountains are draped with purple clouds. No one is allowed near this area.

Once a man went mushroom gathering and found a gold water pipe and a gold dipper deep in the Shiromi mountains. When he tried to lift them, he found that they were too heavy. He tried to chip off the ends of the pipe and the dipper with his sickle, but this didn't work either. Planning to come back later, he cut a notch in a tree to mark the spot. The next day when he came back with others looking for the tree, he could not find it and gave up.

—ᴍ—

34. Along the mountainous area of Shiromi there is a spot called Hanare-mori (detached woods). One small area called the *choja's* house has no one living there. There is a man who sometimes goes there to make charcoal. One night, someone raised the straw mat that hung over the entrance to his hut and peeped in. Inside was a woman with long trailing hair divided down the middle. In this area it is not unusual to hear the screams of women late at night.

—ᴍ—

35. Kizen Sasaki's grandfather's younger brother went to the Shiromi mountains to gather mushrooms and spent the night there. He saw a woman run across in front of a large wooded area on the other side of the valley. It seemed as though she were running through the air. He heard her call out "Just wait" two times.

—ᴍ—

36. Coming across a vicious overaged monkey or wolf is frightening. The mountain Futatsu-ishi (two rocks) near Yamaguchi village is very rocky. One rainy day, some children on their way home from primary school looked up at the mountain and saw wolves crouched on top of the rocks. The wolves, one by one, raised their heads and howled. Seen from the front, they looked like newborn ponies. Seen from behind they appeared unusually small. Nothing is more frightening than the howling of a wolf.

—⁂—

37. It used to be that those who led packhorses between the Sakaigi and Wayama passes would often come across wolves. At night, the packhorse drivers usually formed into groups of ten. Since each man could lead from five to seven horses by a rope, there were often about forty or fifty horses altogether at any one time. Once, two hundred to three hundred wolves came after a group, and the mountain shook just from the sound of their running. Terribly frightened, the men and the horses gathered together, and the men built fires around them for protection. Nevertheless, the wolves still got to them by leaping across the fires. Finally, the drivers removed the ropes from the horses and wrapped them around the group. Then the wolves, seeming to take the ropes for a trap, did not try to jump into the circle any more. The wolves surrounded the group at a distance and howled until daybreak.

—⁂—

38. The head of an old household, who is still living in Otomo village, heard the howling of mean old wolves on his way back from town one day. Being drunk he tried to imitate their call. The wolves seemed to come howling after him. He became frightened and hurried home. He went inside, secured the front door, and hid. The wolves continued to howl around the house throughout the night. At daybreak, he found that the wolves had dug a tunnel under the stable and had devoured seven of his horses. After this, the family fell on hard times.

—m—

39. When still a child, Kizen Sasaki was returning home from the mountains one day with his grandfather when they saw a large deer dead on the bank of a stream near the village. Its side had been ripped open, and the deer could not have been dead very long since vapors still streamed from the wound. His grandfather said, "This is for the wolves to eat. I'd like to have the hide, but a vicious wolf is undoubtedly hiding somewhere nearby, watching us. We can't take it."

—m—

40. It is said that if the grass is nine centimeters long, a wolf can hide in it. Like the changing colors of the plants and trees, the color of the wolf's fur changes with each season.

—m—

41. One year, Kahei Sasaki from Wano went hunting in Oyachi near Sakaigi pass. Oyachi is a flat area extending out from the area of Shisuke. It was late autumn, and the leaves on the trees had already fallen leaving the mountains bare. Suddenly from the opposite peak, Kahei saw countless hundreds of wolves running in a pack toward him. He was filled with fear and climbed to the top of a tree. Below him, he could hear the rumbling of the wolves as they ran off to the north. Ever since then, there has been a decline in the number of wolves in the Tono district.

—m—

42. At the base of Mt. Rokkoushi there are spots named Obaya and Itagoya. These hills are covered with the grass reeds used for making thatched roofs. People from various villages go to cut the reeds. One autumn, when the people from Iide village were cutting reeds, they found three or four young wolves in a rock cave. They killed two and took one back with them. It was from that day on that the wolves began attacking the horses belonging to the people of Iide. However, the wolves did not harm the people or horses of any other villages. The people of Iide met and decided to begin a wolf hunt.

One villager was a wrestler and was quite proud of his strength. He went out onto the field to challenge the wolves, but the male wolves remained in the distance and would not come to fight. When a female wolf came charging out at the man named Tetsu (iron), he took off his jacket, wrapped it around his arm, and then, all at once, thrust his arm into the wolf's mouth. The wolf bit down on his arm. And while thrusting his arm further into the wolf, he called to the others for help, but, frightened, no one would come. By now Tetsu's arm had penetrated to the wolf's stomach and the wolf, in great pain, gnawed down into Tetsu's arm bone. The wolf died on the spot and Tetsu died shortly after being carried away.

—❦—

43. The following article appeared in the local Tono newspaper on May 20, 1906. One snowy day, a man named Kuma (bear) from Kamigo village went hunting on Mt. Rokkoushi with his friend. Deep into the valley they found bear tracks and split up to search for the bear. Kuma went off towards the peak and soon saw a large bear in the shadow of a rock. It was looking in his direction. It was too close for him to fire his rifle, so he put it down and grappled with the bear. They rolled over and over in the snow down into the valley. Kuma's friend wanted to help but wasn't strong enough. Finally, Kuma and the bear fell into a mountain stream, and Kuma sank down into the water beneath the bear. At that moment he killed the bear.

Kuma did not drown. He had been slashed by the bear's claws in several places but managed to survive.

—❦—

44. There is a gold mine on the mountain above the village of Hashino near the peak of Mt. Rokkoushi. The man who makes his living producing charcoal for this mine is also a good flute player. One day, he was in his hut lying on his back playing the flute when someone raised up the straw mat hanging over the entrance to the hut. Surprised, he looked up and saw a vicious old monkey. Frightened, he got up, and the monkey sauntered away.

—❦—

45. Vicious old monkeys are like humans. They become desirous of females and often steal off the village women. They coat their fur with pine resin and then sprinkle sand on it. This makes their fur and skin like armor, and even bullets cannot penetrate it.

---

46. A man who lives at Hayashizaki in Tochinai village is about fifty years old now. This event happened about ten years ago. He went off to shoot deer on Mt. Rokkoushi. When he played his deer-call flute, a vicious old monkey who thought it was a deer headed down from the summit. The monkey, with its large mouth wide open, pushed its way through the bamboo grass. Frightened out of his wits, the man stopped playing his flute, and the monkey ran off in the direction of the valley.

---

47. In this area, children are usually threatened with the words, "The vicious old monkey from Mt. Rokkoushi is going to come!" There are many monkeys on this mountain. If you go Ogase Falls, monkeys are all over the trees on the cliffs. When they see humans, they run off while throwing nuts and things at them.

---

48. There are many monkeys at Sennin-toge (hermit pass). They make fun of people by throwing stones and other things at them.

---

49. It is about nine kilometers up and nine kilometers down from Sennin-toge. Midway up the pass there is a shrine in which the statue of a mountain hermit is worshiped. For a long time, it has been the custom for travelers to write on the shrine walls about the unusual encounters they have had on the mountain. For example, there was "I am from Echigo province, and, on a certain night of a certain month, I met a young girl with trailing hair on this mountain road. She looked at me and smiled." Or there were things such as "I was made fun of by monkeys here" and "I met with three robbers."

---

50. The *kakko* flower blooms on the Shisuke mountains. This flower is rare in the Tono district. In May, when the *kanko-dori* bird sings, girls and children go to the mountains to gather *kakko* flowers. When the flowers are pickled in vinegar, they turn purple. As with the ground cherry, one can play with the *kakko* flower by blowing through it to make sounds. Kids have a great time gathering these flowers.

—⁓—

51. A variety of birds live in the mountains, but the bird with the loneliest voice is the *otto* (husband) bird. It sings on summer nights. It is said that horsepack drivers and others coming over the pass from the seashore at Ozuchi hear this bird down in the bottom of the valley.

Once there was the daughter of a *choja* family who was intimate with the son of another *choja* family. While they were off having fun in the mountains one day, the young man disappeared. From evening until late at night, the girl walked around looking for him, but to no avail. It is said that she eventually became the *otto* bird. The bird's sound, *otto-n, otto-n,* means "my husband, my husband." The bird's voice gradually grows hoarse, and it sounds quite pathetic.

—⁓—

52. The *umaoi-dori* (horse-driving bird) resembles the cuckoo bird, but it is a little larger. Its feathers are red tinged with brown, and its shoulders are striped like the rope used for leading horses. Its breast is marked like the rope used around the horse's nose and mouth.

This bird was once a servant in the home of a *choja*. The servant took horses to the mountain, and, when he started to return home, he found he was missing one horse. He walked around the mountain all night looking for the horse, and finally he turned into the horse-driving bird. In this area the sound *aho, aho* is the sound of someone driving horses in the fields.

In certain years the *umaoi-dori* bird comes to the village and sings. When this happens, it is a sign that there will be a famine.

This sound of this bird can be heard deep in the mountains where it usually lives.

—⚏—

53. The *kakko* (a small dove-like bird) and the cuckoo bird were once sisters. The dove, the elder of the two sisters, dug up a potato and baked it. She ate the hard outer skin of the potato herself and gave the soft inside part to her younger sister. The younger sister thought that the outer skin of the potato that her elder sister had eaten must have been better, and so she killed her sister with a kitchen knife. The elder sister instantly changed into a bird and flew off singing *ganko, ganko*. The sound *ganko* means "the hard part" in the local dialect.

The younger sister, realizing she had actually been given the better part of the potato, was filled with remorse. She too turned into a bird, which, it is said, sings *hocho-kaketa*, which sounds like "cut with a kitchen knife." In Tono, the cuckoo bird is called *hocho-kake*. In Morioka City, the cuckoo bird is said to sing *docha-e-tondeta*, which means "Where did she fly off to?"

—⚏—

54. There are many frightening legends about the numerous deep pools of water in the Hei River. The village of Kawai (rivers meeting) is near where the Hei and Oguni Rivers meet. One day, a servant of a wealthy *choja* family in this village was cutting trees on a hill above one of these deep pools of water when his axe fell off into the water. Since this was his master's axe, he went into the water to search for it. Near the bottom of the pool, he heard a sound. He followed the sound and found a house in the shadows of the rocks. Inside there was a beautiful girl weaving at a loom. His axe was leaning against the loom. He asked if she would return the axe, and, as she turned toward him, he realized that she was his master's daughter, who had died two or three years earlier. She spoke to him saying, "I will return the axe, but don't tell anyone that I am here. In return, I will make you wealthy so that you can live without being a servant."

No one knew the reason, but he had an unusual streak of wins at various forms of gambling. The money piled up, and before long he quit being a servant, stayed home, and became a fairly well-to-do peasant farmer. But he was quite forgetful and did not heed what the master's daughter had told him. One day, when passing the same deep pool of water on his way to town, he recalled the earlier incident and told those with him about what he had seen. Rumors soon spread throughout the area. From then on, his fortune changed and he ended up spending the rest of his life as a servant to his previous master.

No one knew what the master of the household was thinking when he, among other things, kept pouring boiling water into the deep pool. It didn't have any effect.

—⁂—

55. Many *kappa* (mischievous water spirits) live in rivers. There are large numbers of *kappa* in the Saru-ga-ishi River. In a house by the river in Matsuzaki village, women have become pregnant with a *kappa's* children for two generations. When the *kappa*-children are born, they are hacked into pieces, put into small wine casks, and buried in the ground. They are grotesque.

The home of a woman's husband was in Niibari village. This house was also beside a river. The head of the family told people the following facts. "One day a whole family went into the fields. In the evening when they were about to return home, they found a woman crouching beside the river smiling. The next day during the noon break the same thing happened again. This happened day after day, and gradually the rumor spread that someone from the village was visiting the woman at night. At first, the visits were only when her husband was away driving packhorses to the seaside. Later the visits were made even when she was sleeping beside her husband. Over time, it became evident that the visitor must be a *kappa*, and so all the relatives gathered together to protect the woman. This too failed. The husband's mother also went and slept at the wife's side. Late at night when she heard the wife laughing and knew that the visitor had come, she found it impossible to move her body. There was nothing anyone could do."

The woman had great difficulty giving birth, and someone suggested that if they filled the tub that horses ate from with water and put her in it, this would ease the delivery. They tried this, and it worked. The child had webbed hands. It is said that the mother of this woman had also given birth to the child of a *kappa*.

Some people say such an occurrence is fate and is not limited to two or three generations. This family was wealthy and had an elite warrior-class surname. They had even been members of the village association.

—∞—

56. A child looking something like a *kappa* was born into a certain family in Kamigo village. There was no definite proof that it was a *kappa's* child, but it had bright red skin and a large mouth. It was indeed a disgusting child. Loathing the child and wanting to get rid of it, someone took it to a fork in the road and sat it down. After having walked away only a short distance, he realized that he could make money by showing it. He went back, but it was already hiding and nowhere to be seen.

—∞—

57. It's not unusual to see the footprints of *kappa* in the sand along the bank of a river. This is especially true on the day after it rains. A *kappa's* foot, just like that of a monkey, has the large toe separated off. It is like the handprint of a human being. The print is less than eight centimeters in length. It is said that the tip of the *kappa's* toe doesn't leave the distinct mark that a human toe does.

—∞—

58. Near the Obako deepwater pool of the Kogarase River there is a home called the New House. One day a child took a horse to cool off in the deep pool and then went off to play. A *kappa* appeared and tried to pull the horse deeper into the water, but instead the *kappa* was pulled out of the water by the horse and dragged off to the stable. The *kappa* hid under the horse's feed bucket.

Someone thought it strange that the feed bucket was upside down, and when they tilted it back a *kappa's* hand came out. All of the villagers gathered to discuss whether to kill the kappa or release it. They decided to let it go with a firm promise from the *kappa* that henceforth it would not make mischief with the village horses. This *kappa* has now left the village and is said to be living in a deep pool at Aizawa Falls.[1]

1. Folktale variations of this legend can be found throughout Japan.

—※—

59. In other areas, the *kappa's* face is said to be green, but in Tono the *kappa's* face is red. When she was young, Kizen Sasaki's great-grandmother was playing with friends in the garden when she saw a boy with a dark red face behind three walnut trees. It was a *kappa*. Those big walnut trees are still there. The area around the house is now filled with walnut trees.

—※—

60. An old man named Kahei from Wano village was in a pheasant hunting blind waiting for the birds to appear. A fox kept coming out, scaring off the pheasant. Kahei got angry and decided to shoot the fox, but when he took aim, the fox turned toward him and looked at him indifferently. He pulled the trigger, but his gun didn't fire. Upset, he examined the rifle only to find that, without his knowing it, the barrel had been filled from one end to the other with dirt.

—※—

61. The same hunter went to Mt. Rokkoushi and came across a white deer. There is the story that the white deer is a spirit or *kami*. He figured that if he only wounded the deer, and did not kill it, he would surely be cursed. Being a famous hunter and disliking social criticism, he resolved to shoot the deer. He shot and was sure he had hit it, but the deer didn't move. Upset by this, he took out a gold bullet that he usually carried to ward off evil or for use in a crisis. He wrapped mugwort around the bullet and fired, but the deer, as before, didn't move.

Thinking this strange, he moved closer to look. He found a white rock that closely resembled the shape of a deer. He had lived in the mountains for decades and thought he could surely tell the difference between a rock and a deer! He felt this had to be the doings of some evil spirit. It is said that this was the only time he considered giving up hunting.

—⚬—

62. Again, the same man was in the mountains one night, and not having time to construct a hut, he took shelter under a large tree. He wrapped a rope used to ward off evil around himself and the tree three times. He dozed off with his arm around his gun. Late at night, he was stirred by a noise and saw something shaped like a huge priest hovering over the top of the tree flapping its red robe-like wings. He shouted, "Heavens!" and fired his gun. The figure flapped its wings again and flew off. He was really frightened. He had this unusual experience three times. Each time, he would promise to give up hunting and prayed to the family spirit. But then, he would reconsider and tell people that he would find it impossible to give up hunting until he grew old.

—⚬—

63. Mr. Miura of Oguni is the richest man in the village. Two or three generations earlier, the household was poor and the master's wife was rather stupid. One day, the wife went gathering butterbur herbs along the small stream that flowed in front of the gate. Because there were not many good plants there, she went further into the valley. All of a sudden, she looked up, and there was a house with a splendid black gate. She entered the gate hesitantly and saw a large garden with red and white flowers blooming with many hens running about. Toward the back of the garden there was a shed with many cows and a stable with many horses. But there were no people. Finally, she entered the house through the main entrance, and in the next room she found many red and black serving trays and bowls set out. In the inner room there was a charcoal fire and an iron pot with the water boiling briskly. Nevertheless, there was not a trace of anyone. Thinking that this might be the home of a mountain man, she became frightened and ran home. She told people about what she had seen, but no one would believe her.

Again, another day while she was washing things on the bank of the stream in front of the gate, a red bowl came floating down from upstream. Because it was so beautiful she lifted it out of the water. Thinking that she might be scolded if she used this unclean bowl as tableware, she put it into the grain box and used it to measure rice. As soon as she began to measure grain with this bowl, the grain never decreased in volume. The family thought this phenomenon strange, and when they asked her the reason, she told them for the first time how she had picked the bowl out of the stream. From then on the household had good fortune, and it became the Miura family of today.

In Tono, a strange house in the mountains is called a *mayoi-ga* (a house found when one loses their way). Anyone who finds a *mayoi-ga* is permitted to take anything they like from among the household objects and domestic animals. The house appears in order to give the person good fortune. It is believed that because the woman was not greedy and did not steal anything from the house when she first found it, the red bowl came floating down the river to her of its own accord.

—◊—

64. Kanesawa village, which is at the foot of the Shiromi mountains, is especially deep in the mountains for the Kamihei region, so few people travel through the village. Six or seven years ago a man from this village was adopted to marry the daughter of a family at Yamazaki in Tochinai village. The man got lost on a mountain path one day on his way back to his original family. He also came across a *mayoi-ga*. The appearance of the house, the numerous cows, horses and hens, the blooming red and white flowers—everything was the same as in the previous story. In the same way, he entered the main entrance, and the red and black serving trays and bowls were set out. The inner room had a tea kettle with the water boiling briskly, and it appeared as if someone was about to make tea. He thought that there must be someone in the bathroom or somewhere around. At first he was dazed, but then he grew more and more terrified. He left the house and finally went back to Oguni village. In Oguni village nobody believed his story when they heard it, but in Yamazaki the people thought what he explained had to be a *mayoi-ga*. They

thought that if they went and brought back the serving trays or bowls they would become wealthy *choja*. The husband took the lead, and they all went back into the mountains in search of the house. They came to the spot where he said the gate had been, but there was nothing to be seen, and they returned home empty-handed. Nothing was ever heard of the husband becoming rich.

—⁂—

65. Mt. Hayachine is a granite mountain. On the side of the mountain that faces Oguni there is a rock called Abe Castle. The rock is halfway up a steep cliff, and it is not easy to get there. It is said that even now the mother of Abe-no-Sadato lives there.[1] On nights when it rains, it is said that one can hear the sound of the door on the cave being shut. The people in Oguni and Tsukumoushi say that it is the sound of the lock of Abe Castle. They say that when this sound is made it will rain the next day.

1. The Abe family is mentioned in legend 26. Abe-no-Sadato (1019–1062), the son of Abe-no-Yoritoki (d. 1057), received territory in the Tono (Iwate) region from his father and fought a number of battles there. He fought with Minamoto-no-Yoshiie (1039–1106), mentioned in the next legend as Hachiman Taro.

—⁂—

66. On the Tsukumoushi side of the same mountain, at the entrance for climbing, there is also a rocky cave called the Abe Residence. It is known that Abe-no-Sadato was closely associated with Mt. Hayachine. At the starting point for the ascent of Mt. Hayachine on the Oguni side, there are three earthen mounds. These mounds are said to be the graves of Hachiman Taro's soldiers, who died in battle.

—⁂—

67. There are many other legends about Abe-no-Sadato. There is a vast plain about ten kilometers back in the mountains from Yamaguchi on the border between Tsuchibuchi village and Kurihashi village (once called Hashino). In that area there is a place called Sadato.

There is a marsh there, and it is said Abe-no-Sadato brought his horses there to cool off. Some also say that this is where Sadato made his military camp. The scenery of the area is beautiful, and the eastern coastline is visible from there.

—✠—

68. The Abe household in Tsuchibuchi village is said to have descended from Abe-no-Sadato. At one time the family was very prosperous. Even now there is a moat with water surrounding the house. There are numerous swords and elaborate horse harnesses in the house. The present household head, Yoemon Abe, is the second or third wealthiest man in the village and a member of the village assembly.

There are many other descendants of Abe family. Some are in the vicinity of the Abe fortress in Morioka City. One family is near the bamboo water-retaining wall on the Kuriya River. There are the remains of a fortress at a bend in the Kogarase River, some four hundred meters north of the Abe house in Tsuchibuchi village. It is called Hachiman-zawa fortress, and it is said that this is where Hachiman Taro once made his camp. From here, on the road to the town of Tono, there is a mountain called Mt. Hachiman. On the summit, facing the Hachiman-zawa fortress, there are the remains of another fortress. This is said to be where Abe-no-Sadato made his camp. These two fortresses are about three kilometers apart. There are tales of bow and arrow battles between the two fortresses, and lots of arrowheads have been dug up in the area. Between these two fortresses there is the village of Nitakai. At the time of the battles, this area was filled with reeds. The soil being soft and watery, it would give way and move. One time when Hachiman Taro was going through this area, he saw how the troops on both sides had plenty of rice gruel (kayu), and he said, "So this is nita-kayu [hot rice gruel] is it?" Nitakai became the village name.

The small river flowing just beyond Nitakai village is called the Naru River. On the other side of the river there is the village of Ashiraga (Foot-Washing River). It is said that the name of the village comes from the fact that Hachiman Taro washed his feet in the Naru River.

—✠—

69. In Tsuchibuchi village there are currently two households called *daido*. Mannojo Ohora is the current head of the *daido* in Yamaguchi. His mother-in-law, named Ohide, is over eighty, and she is still healthy. She is Kizen Sasaki's grandmother's elder sister. She is a master of witchcraft. She has shown Kizen Sasaki how she can cast a spell to kill a snake or drop a bird perched in a tree. Last year, on January 15 by the old calendar, the old woman told this story: "Once upon a time there was a poor farmer. He had no wife but did have a beautiful daughter. He also had one horse. The daughter loved the horse, and at night she would go to the stable and sleep. She and the horse eventually became husband and wife. One night the father learned of this. The next day without saying anything to the daughter, he took the horse out and killed it by hanging it from a mulberry tree. That night the daughter asked her father why the horse was not anywhere around, and she found out what he had done. Shocked and filled with grief, she went to the spot beneath the mulberry tree and cried while clinging to the horse's head. The

Oshira-sama

father, disgusted, took an axe and chopped off the horse's head from behind. Then, the daughter, clinging to the horse's head, flew off into the sky. It was from this time on that Oshira-sama became a *kami* (deity). The image of this *kami* is made from the mulberry branch on which the horse was hanged. There are three of these images. The one made from the larger end of the branch is in the *daido* household of Yamaguchi. This is the elder sister *kami*. The image made from the center of the branch was in the house of a commoner named Gonjuro in Yamazaki. Kizen Sasaki's aunt married into that family, but now the household has died out, and the whereabouts of that *kami* aren't known. The younger sister *kami* image was made from the smaller end of the branch and is said to be in Tsukumoushi village now."

—⊶—

70. The same old woman says that the Okunai-sama deity is always present in households that have the Oshira-sama *kami*. Nevertheless, there are some households where there is no Oshira-sama and only an Okunai-sama. And depending upon the family, the images of the two *kami* are different. The Okunai-sama in the *daido* family of Yamaguchi is a wooden image. The Okunai-sama in Tanie Haneishi's house in Yamaguchi is a paper scroll. The one in the well-to-do Abe household in Kashiwazaki is also a wooden image. In the *daido* household of Iide, they have no Oshira-sama, but they do have an Okunai-sama.

—⊶—

71. The old woman who related this story is an avid devotee of the Amida Buddha, but she is different from the usual believer in the Amida Buddha. Her belief is a kind of heretical one. She informs believers in the ways of the faith, and they all maintain a strict secrecy about it. They do not even inform their parents or children about these rules and techniques. This group has no relation to established Buddhist temples or priests. It is a gathering of ordinary peasants. There are not many followers. The woman Tanie Haneishi is a member of this group. On special days of observance for the Amida

Buddha, this group waits until everyone is asleep, and late at night they meet and offer up prayers in a hidden room. They are skilled at sorcery and incantations and have some power in the village.

—⚉—

72. The area called Kotobata in Tochinai village is in a swamp deep in the mountains. There are only five houses in this area, which is on the upper reaches of a tributary of the Kogarase River. It is about seven kilometers from here to the dwellings in Tochinai. There is an earth mound at the entrance to Kotobata, and on the mound is a seated sculpture made of wood. This image is about the size of a person. It used to be inside a shrine, but now it is in the open and exposed to the rain. The people call it Kakura-sama. The children make a plaything of the image by pulling it down and throwing it into the river or dragging it along the road. Now the nose and mouth are no longer distinguishable. If anyone scolds the children for this or restrains them from playing with the sculpture, it is said a curse will be cast on them and they will become sick.[1]

1. Gods (*kami*) and Buddhist figures like to play with children and get angry if someone tries to interfere. Kakura-sama protects the entrance to the village.

—⚉—

73. There are many wooden images of Kakura-sama in the Tono district. There are also some in Nishi-nai village in Tochinai. Some people also remember seeing images at a place called Ohora in Yamaguchi. Kakura-sama is not worshiped by people. It is crudely carved, and its robes and head decorations are not very distinct.

—⚉—

74. The Kakura-sama of Tochinai, mentioned above, can be either large or small. One village in Tsuchibuchi has three or four of these images. No matter which Kakura-sama it is, it is a wooden image in a sitting position roughly hewn and undefined. Still, it is possible to discern that it has a face like a person. Kakura-sama used to be the name of a spot where deities would rest while on a journey. Now this spot is referred to as Kakura-sama.

—⚉—

75. Up until a few years ago, there was a small matchstick factory on a *choja's* property in Hanaremori. After dark, a woman would come to the doorway of the shed, look at the people, and laugh in a scary, vulgar way. The workers couldn't stand the isolation of this location, and the factory was finally moved to Yamaguchi. Later, again in the same mountain area, someone set up a hut for cutting wood for railroad ties. One night a laborer strayed off, and, after coming back, he remained in a dazed state for some time. After this incident, four or five other workers kept going off to somewhere. Later, they said that a woman came and led them off somewhere. It is said that after returning, they could not remember anything for two or three days.

—ɯ—

76. The term *choja-yashiki* refers to the remains of a house where a wealthy farmer once lived. There is also a hill there called *nuka-mori* (rice-bran forest). It is said that this hill was made from the rice husks thrown away by the *choja* family. There is a five-leafed *utsugi* bush with white flowers on this hill, and it is said that there is gold buried under the tree. Even now, one sometimes hears of people searching for the location of this *utsugi* bush. This *choja* family was perhaps at one time connected with a gold mine. There is still iron slag from refining in the area. Not too far off on a nearby mountain there is the Ondoku gold mine.

—ɯ—

77. Chozaburo Tajiri of Yamaguchi was the wealthiest man in Tsuchibuchi village. According to the aged head of this family, when he was a little over forty, the son of old Ohide died. On the night of the funeral, after everyone had finished their prayers to Amida Buddha, Chozaburo, being a talkative type, lingered behind. When he got up to leave, there was a man sleeping under the eaves, using a stone at the base of the drainpipe as a pillow. Chozaburo looked closely, but he did not know the man, who seemed to be dead. It was a moonlit night, and in that light the man seemed to be on his back with his knees pulled up and his mouth open. Being a bold fellow, Chozaburo nudged the fellow with his foot, but the man didn't

move. The man was blocking the path, and since there was no other way to go, he stepped over him and went home.

Chozaburo went back to the same spot the next morning, but naturally there was not a trace of the man, and no one else had seen anything. The shape and location of the rock used as a pillow was just as Chozaburo had remembered it from the night before. He said that he should have touched the man with his hand, but because he was somewhat frightened, he only nudged him with his foot. He couldn't imagine what was going on.

—m—

78. According to the same person, a servant named Chozo from Yamaguchi is now over seventy years of age and lives there. One night, he went out for some fun and was coming back late when in front of his master's gate, which stood facing the Ozuchi highway, he saw a person coming from the coast. The person was wearing a straw snow cape. As the man drew near and then stopped, Chozo, somewhat suspicious, watched him. The man crossed over the road and shot off in the direction of the fields. Chozo thought there was a hedge there, and looking carefully, sure enough there it was! All of a sudden he became terrified, ran into the house, and told his master what had happened. Later he heard that at the same moment he

Tono L-shaped Farm House

had seen the stranger, someone from Niihari village had fallen off their horse and died while on the way back from the coast.

—⚉—

79. Chozo's father was also called Chozo. They had been servants in the Tajiri household for generations. Chozo and his wife worked together. When he was young, Chozo went out to enjoy himself one evening and came back just after sundown. Just as he entered the gate, he saw the shadow of a man near the side entrance. The man stood with his arms folded inside his jacket. His empty sleeves hung down. His face was indistinct and could not be seen.

Chozo's wife was named Otsune. Thinking that this fellow had come to court Otsune, Chozo went straight toward him. The man did not run around to the back but instead went to the main front entrance just off to the right. Chozo thought, "You're not going to make a fool of me." He got angry and went after him. The man stepped back with his arms still folded and gently slipped inside through the wooden entrance doors, which were open a mere nine centimeters. Chozo, still not thinking anything unusual, stuck his hand into the opening in the entrance doors and felt around in-

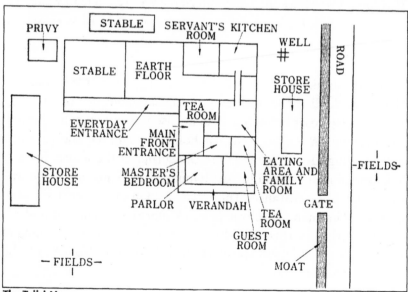

The Tajiri House

side. The sliding, paper-covered doors further on the inside were closed.

With this, he now became frightened. He drew back a little and then looked up. The man was flat against the wall above the entrance looking down at Chozo. The man's head hung down and almost touched Chozo's. The man's eyeballs were about thirty centimeters in size and seemed to pop out. This was a terrible moment, but it did not prove to be a warning of any kind.

—ɯ—

80. To understand the story above, it is necessary to diagram the layout of the Tajiri house. Houses in the Tono area are built more or less the same as in this diagram.

The main gate of the Tajiri house faces north, but the gate usually faces east. This means that in the diagram, the gate would usually be where the stable is. The main gate is called *jomae* (castle front). There are fields all around the housing compound, but there is no fence or wall. Between the master's bedroom and the family room, there is a small dark room called the *zato-beya* (blind man's room). Years ago, when they had a party, the family always had blind entertainers (*zato*). This room was where the blind entertainers were made to wait.[1]

1. Tono houses are called *magariya* ("bent" or "L-shaped"). The stable for horses is part of the house.

—ɯ—

81. At Nozaki in Tochinai there was a man named Mankichi Maekawa. He died two or three years ago at about the age of thirty. Two or three years before he died, he also was out enjoying himself one evening. When he returned home, he entered the gate and walked alongside the verandah to the corner of the house. It was a June, moonlit night, and he just happened to glance up at the wall above the front entrance. There was a man flat against the wall sleeping. The man's face was pale. Mankichi was shocked and got sick. Nevertheless, this time also, the incident was not a warning of any kind. Mr. Tajiri's son Marukichi heard this story from Mankichi, who is his good friend.

—ɯ—

82. This story is about something a man named Marukichi Tajiri experienced. One night when he was young, he left the family room on the way to the toilet. As he entered the tearoom, he saw someone standing at the edge of the parlor. The shape was indistinct, but even in the darkness the stripes on the clothing and the man's eyes and nose were visible. His hair hung down.

Marukichi was frightened, but reached out with his hand to feel the way and bumped into the door. He could feel the door, but couldn't see his own hand. He looked up and there was something like a shadow in the form of a person. When he put his hand on the spot where the face was, the face could then be seen on top of his hand.

He went back to the family room and told people about it. When he took the paper-covered lantern to look at the spot again, there was nothing there. Marukichi is a very modern and intelligent person and he is not the kind of person to tell a lie.

—☓—

83. The house of Mannojo Ohora, a *daido* of Yamaguchi, is built a little different from other houses. It is laid out as in the diagram.

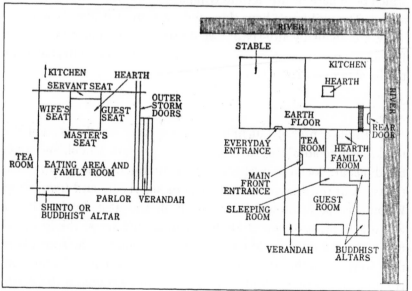

The Mannojo Ohora House

The main entrance faces toward the southeast. It is a very old house. If anyone opens the wicker trunk in the house and looks at the old documents there, they will be cursed.

—⸹—

84. Three or four years ago Kizen Sasaki's grandfather was just about seventy when he died. He was probably in his teens during the 1850s when many Westerners came to live in areas along the coast. There were Western-style buildings in Kamaishi and Yamada. A Westerner even once lived on a promontory on Funakoshi Peninsula. Christianity was practiced secretly, and in the Tono district believers were crucified. According to those who visit the ports on the coast, there are still old people who talk of the *ijin* (foreigners) embracing and kissing. It is said there are quite a few multiracial children in the coastal areas.[1]

1. European ships visited the coastal areas near Tono beginning in the early 1600s.

—⸹—

85. At Kashiwazaki in Tsuchibuchi village there is a household in which both parents are definitely Japanese, but the two children are albino. The children's hair, skin, and eyes are just like Westerners. They are about twenty-six or twenty-seven years old now and are farming. Their pronunciation and accents are also different from the local people. Their voices are high and piercing.

—⸹—

86. In the center of Tsuchibuchi village there is a place called Motojuku, where administrative offices, the primary school, and other buildings are located. In this area, a man named Masa, now about thirty-six or thirty-seven years old, runs a soybean-curd (*tofu*) shop. When this man's father was seriously ill and near death, a house was under construction at Shimo-Tochinai just across the Kogarase River. Toward evening, Masa's father came alone to the spot where they were pounding the earth to harden up the house foundation. He greeted everyone, said that he ought to help pound the earth, and joined in and worked. After a while, it got dark, and he returned

home with everyone. Later, people thought this was a little strange since the man was supposed to be very sick. Later they heard that he had died on that very day.

People went to pay their respects and told about what had happened on the day Masa's father died. It was exactly at that time that the sick person had breathed his last breath.

—៣—

87. I have forgotten the person's name, but he was from a wealthy family in the town of Tono. He was seriously ill and on the brink of death, when one day he suddenly visited a Buddhist temple. The temple priest entertained him courteously and served tea. They chatted about things, and then the priest, somewhat suspicious when the man was about to leave, sent his younger disciple to follow him. The man went out the gate and headed in the direction of home. Then he went around a corner in the town and disappeared. There were other people who met him on that street and he greeted everyone as politely as ever.

The man died that night, and, of course, he was in no condition

Stone Monuments to Mountain Gods

to be going out at that time. Later at the temple, the priest checked the spot where the man's teacup had been placed to see if his tea had been drunk. He found that all of the tea had been poured into a crack between the straw mats.

—៣—

88. This story is similar to the one before. The Jokenji Temple in Tsuchibuchi of Tsuchibuchi village belongs to the Soto sect of Buddhism and ranks first among the twelve temples in the Tono district. One evening,

a villager met an old man on the road coming from Motojuku. This old man had been seriously ill for some time, and when the villager asked when he had gotten better, he replied that he had felt fine for two or three days. Today, he was on his way to hear a sermon at the temple. In front of the temple gate they spoke again and parted. At Jokenji Temple as well, the priest came to welcome the old man who had come to visit. Tea was served, they chatted for a while, and the old man left. Again a young temple disciple was sent after the man to watch him, and the old man disappeared outside the temple gate. Surprised, the young disciple told the priest about this. Again the tea had been poured between the straw mats. The old man died on that day.

—ɯ—

89. To go to Kashiwazaki from Yamaguchi, you have to go around the base of Mt. Atago. Along the way there are rice fields and then pine trees. From the spot where one can see the houses of Kashiwazaki, there are thickets of bushes and small trees.

There is a small shrine on the top of Mt. Atago. A path for people coming to worship goes through a wood. There is a sacred Shinto gate and about twenty or thirty old cedar trees at the entrance to the mountain. Next to this, there is an empty shrine. In front of this shrine, there is a stone monument with the words "mountain deity (kami)" carved into it. It has been said since olden times that this is the spot where the mountain kami appears.

A youth from Wano had some business in Kashiwazaki, and in the evening, when passing by the empty shrine, he saw a tall man coming down from the top of Mt. Atago. Wondering who it might be, the youth approached and looked at the person's face, which appeared above a cluster of trees. At the bend in the road the two met unexpectedly. The tall man, unsuspecting, was quite surprised. The face looking at the youth was bright red, had radiant eyes, and indeed contained an expression of surprise. The youth knew it had to be the mountain kami, and he ran off to Kashiwazaki without ever looking back.[1]

1. There are numerous stone monuments to the mountain kami in the Tono district. These are found at locations where someone met or was cursed by a mountain kami. These monu-

ments are set up to pacify the *kami*. Mountain *kami* can be male or female and sometimes give people special powers.

—𝕞—

90. There is a hill called *Tengu-mori* (forest of the long-nosed goblins) in Matsuzaki village.[1] A young man from the village was working in the mulberry fields at the foot of the hill when he became very sleepy. He sat down on the narrow footpath between the fields for a while, and as he started to doze off, a very large man with a bright red face came up. The youth, rather easygoing and usually fond of sports like wrestling, didn't like the look of this large stranger standing astride the path looking down at him. He jumped up and asked, "Where did you come from?" There was no reply. He thought he would push the large man away, and, confident of his strength, the youth was just about to spring at and grapple with the large man when he was thrown and lost consciousness. In the evening when he recovered and looked around, of course, the large man was no longer there. The young man returned home and told people about his experience.

That autumn, this same youth went to Mt. Hayachine leading horses with many other villagers to cut bush clover. When they were about to return only the youth was missing. Everyone was surprised, and they searched for him. It is said that he died deep in the valley, ripped limb from limb. This was about twenty or thirty years ago and some old people are still around who remember the events of the time. Since olden times, people have believed that a large number of *tengu* reside in *Tengu-mori*.

1. *Tengu* are long-nosed, red-faced creatures that appear half-human and half-bird-like. They are deities of the mountain.

—𝕞—

91. There is a man in the town of Tono who is knowledgeable about the mountains. At one time, he was in charge of the falcons of the ruler Baron Nambu. The people in the town call this man by the nickname Torigozen, which means "Bird Keeper." He knows the shape and location of every tree and rock on both Mt. Hayachine and Mt. Rokkoushi. When he was old, he went gathering mushrooms

with a companion. The companion, who was an excellent swimmer, had the reputation of being able to go into the water with some straw and a hand mallet and come out with straw sandals made.

These two men went to the hill, Mukaiyama, which is across the Saru-ga-ishi River from the town of Tono. From there, they went into the mountains just a little higher up than the spot with unusual rocks. This spot is known as Tsuzuki-ishi, in Ayaori village. The two men separated, and Torigozen went just a little higher up the mountain. The light of the autumn sky lingered just above the western hills, as it does around four o'clock in the afternoon. Suddenly in the shadow of a huge rock, he came across a red-faced man and woman standing and talking. They watched Torigozen approach and then stretched out their hands as if to press him back or restrain him. But he went on regardless, and the woman seemed to cling to the man's chest. From the way they looked, Torigozen did not think they were humans. Being a playful type, he drew out the long knife at his side and struck at them. The red-faced man raised his leg as if to kick, and that is the last thing that Torigozen remembered.

The companion looked around for Torigozen and found him unconscious at the bottom of the valley. He was cared for and taken home. Torigozen told all of the details of the day and how he had never before experienced such a thing. He said, "I might have died. Don't tell anyone else about this."

He was sick for about three days and died. Family members thought that the way he died was somewhat strange and went to consult with the roving priest named Kenko-in. He told them that because Torigozen had disturbed the place where the mountain *kami* were playing, he had been cursed and died. This man was an acquaintance of the scholar Kanori Ino and others.[1] The incident took place over ten years ago.

1. Yanagita met with the local scholar Kanori Ino (1867–1925) during his trip to Tono in 1909. Yanagita knew of Ino's writings and consulted with him about Tono local history and customs.

—ᴍ—

92. This happened last year. About fourteen or fifteen children, from a place in Tsuchibuchi village, went to play on Mt. Hayachine. Before

they knew it, evening had approached, and as they hurried down toward the foot of the mountain, they met a tall man rushing up the mountain. He was dark and had bright glittering eyes. He had a small bundle on his back wrapped in old, light blue cloth, probably linen. As frightened as they were, one of the children spoke up and said, "Where are you headed?" to which came the reply, "I'm going toward Oguni."

This was not the right path for going to Oguni, and the children paused, somewhat puzzled. No sooner had the man passed than he immediately disappeared. It is said they all ran home screaming, "A mountain man! A mountain man!"

—⚬—

93. The wife of Kikuzo Kikuchi of Wano comes from Hashino, which is on the other side of Fuefuki-toge (flute-blowing pass). While his wife was away in her native village her son Itozo, who was five or six years old, became sick.

It was early afternoon when Kikuzo passed over Fuefuki-toge on his way to his wife's village to bring her home. There was a well-known ridge on Mt. Rokkoushi, and the mountain path was thick with trees. Especially in the area going down to Kurihashi from Tono, there were steep cliffs on both sides of the path. The sun sank down behind the cliff, and it was getting dark when someone called out "Kikuzo!" from behind. He turned around and saw someone looking down from the top of the cliff. His face was red and his eyes were bright and radiant—just as in the previous story. The man said, "Your child is already dead." When Kikuzo heard these words, before he could be frightened, he thought, "Oh! It must be so!" The figure on top of the cliff disappeared.

Kikuzo and his wife hurried home throughout the night, but, as they feared, their child was already dead. This happened four or five years ago.

—⚬—

94. This same Kikuzo went to his sister's house in Kashiwazaki to do something. When he left her house, he put some rice cakes that had been left over into his jacket. Just as he passed the woods at the base of Mt. Atago, he met his good friend Toshichi of Zotsubo, who

was quite a drinker. They were in the woods, but there were some grassy areas. Toshichi smiled and pointing to a grassy spot said, "How about wrestling here a bit?" Kikuzo thought it a good idea, and they spent some time wrestling on the grass. But Toshichi seemed weak and so light as to be easily grappled with and thrown. It was such fun that they did it three times. Toshichi said, "I'm no match for you today. I'd better be going." They parted. After Kikuzo had gone only several meters, he noticed that his rice cakes were gone. He went back to where they had wrestled and looked around, but they were not there.

For the first time, he thought, "I wonder if Toshichi was really a fox." Since he was ashamed of what others would say, he didn't mention it to anyone. Four or five days later he went to a wine store and met Toshichi. Kikuzo told him of his experience and Toshichi said, "I wrestled with you? No way, I was at the coast that day." At last it was clear that Kikuzo had wrestled with a fox. He kept it a secret, but last year during the New Year's holiday, when everyone was drinking, the topic of foxes came up. He told what had happened and was really laughed at.

—⚬—

95. A man named Kikuchi from Matsuzaki, who this year is about forty-three or forty-four, is very good at designing gardens. He would go into the mountains, dig up plants and flowers, and then plant them in his own garden. Whenever he found an unusually shaped rock, he would carry it back to his house irrespective of its weight.

One day, not feeling too good, he went out to relax in the hills. He found a beautiful large rock unlike anything he had ever seen before. Since it was his hobby, he thought he would take it home with him, but upon trying to lift it he found it too heavy. It was shaped like a person standing and was about as tall as a person. Really wanting it, he lifted it onto his back and walked several meters with difficulty. It was so heavy that he began to feel faint. He put the rock by the side of the road, and when he leaned against it, he felt as if he were being swept away into the sky along with the rock. It seemed as though he was above the clouds in a very bright and pure place with many kinds of flowers blooming. Off somewhere, he could hear the voices of a large number of people.

The rock rose higher and higher, and just when he thought it had finished rising, he lost consciousness. After some time had passed, he noticed that he was still leaning against this unusual rock, just as before. Not sure what might happen if he took the rock back to his house, he got frightened and ran home. The rock is still in the same spot. He says that whenever he sees it, he still wants to have it.

—⚭—

96. In Tono there was a retarded man about thirty-five or thirty-six years old named Yoshiko the Fool. He was alive until two years ago. He had the habit of picking up pieces of wood from the road, and he would then twist them, stare at them, and smell them. When he went to someone's home, he would rub the supporting wooden pillars and then smell his hands. No matter what it was, he would bring it up close to his eyes, and, while grinning, he would sniff it over and over.

When walking around, he would sometimes suddenly stop, pick up a rock or something, and then throw it at a nearby house screaming loudly "Fire!" Whenever he did this, that night or on the next day, the house that had been hit by the object would catch fire. When this happened a number of times, people got cautious and took preventive measures. But in the end, all the houses caught fire.

—⚭—

97. Matsunojo Kikuchi of Iide was ill with an acute fever from exposure to the cold and would often lose his breath. He went out into the rice fields and hurried off to the family temple of Kisei-in. When he would put a little force into his legs, he could fly into the air about as high as a person's head and then gradually glide down. Again with a little effort, he could fly up. There are no words to express how much fun he was having.

As be approached the temple gate, he saw a crowd of people. Wondering what could be going on, he entered the gate, and there were red poppies in full bloom as far as one could see. He felt better than ever before. His dead father was standing amid the flowers and asked, "Have you come too?" While somehow answering, he moved on. A son he had lost earlier was there and also asked, "Papa, have you come too?" Matsunojo drew closer saying, "Is this where you have been?" The child said, "You can't come now!" At that moment someone by the gate called out Matsunojo's name loudly. As troublesome as it was, he paused reluctantly, and, with a heavy heart, decided to turn back. Then he regained his senses. His relatives had gathered around and were throwing water on him to call him back to life.

---

98. It is quite common to find large rocks by the side of the road with the words "mountain *kami* (deity)," "*kami* of the fields," and "*kami* of the village entrance" engraved on them. There are also rocks in the Tono district with the names Mt. Hayachine and Mt. Rokkoushi engraved in them. Rocks like this are more numerous along the coast.

---

99. Kiyoshi Kitagawa, an assistant headman in Tsuchi-buchi village, lived in Hiishi. His family had been roving priests for generations. His grandfather, named Seifuku-in, was a scholar who had written many books and done a lot for the village. Kiyoshi's younger brother Fukuji married into a family in Tanohama on the coast. Fukuji lost his wife and one of his children in the tidal wave that struck the area last year.[1] For about a year, he was with the two children who survived in a shelter set up on the site of the original house.

On a moonlit night in early summer, he got up to go to the toilet. It was off at some distance where the waves broke on the path by the beach. This night, the fog hovered low, and he saw two people, a man and a woman, approaching him through the fog. The woman was definitely his wife who had died. Without thinking, he trailed after them to a cavern on the promontory in the direction of Funakoshi village. When he called out his wife's name, she looked back and smiled. The man he saw was from the same village, and he too had died in the tidal wave disaster. It had been rumored that this man and Fukuji's wife had been deeply in love before Fukuji had been picked to marry her.

She said, "I am now married to this man." Fukuji replied, "But don't you love your children?" The color of her face changed slightly and she cried. Fukuji didn't realize that he was talking with the dead. While he was looking down at his feet feeling sad and miserable, the man and the woman moved on quickly and disappeared around the mountain on the way to Oura. He tried to run after them and then suddenly realized they were the dead. He stood on the road thinking until daybreak and went home in the morning. It is said that he was sick for a long time after this.

1. The northeastern coast of Japan was struck by tidal waves seven times between 1600 and 1850. The reference in this legend is to a tidal wave that struck the coast in 1896. About nine thousand homes were destroyed, and twenty thousand people died.

—⚬⚬—

100. A certain fisherman at Funakoshi was on his way back from Kirikiri with his companions one day. Late at night, as they were passing by the area of the Forty-Eight Hills, they came across a woman alone by a stream. The fisherman looked and realized that it was his wife. He figured that there was no reason for her coming to this area alone in the middle of the night and decided that it had to be a ghost creature of some kind. At once, he took out the knife that he used to clean fish and stabbed her from behind. She gave out a sorrowful cry and died. Since she didn't reveal her true form right away, he began to feel uneasy. He asked his companions to look after everything and said he was going to hurry home. His wife was safe at home waiting. She said, "I just had a terrible dream. In my dream, I went out partway to meet you since you were rather late in returning. On a mountain path I was threatened by someone I didn't know and thought he was going to kill me. Then I woke up."

At last he understood. When he returned to the previous place, he found that the woman he had killed in the mountains had changed into a fox right before his companions. It is thought that in dreams people sometimes take on the form of this animal in order to go into the fields or mountains.

—⚬⚬—

101. A traveler was passing through Toyomane village late one night. Being tired, it was fortunate that he saw a light in a friend's house. When he stopped in and asked if he could rest there, the friend replied, "You have come at just the right moment. Someone died this evening, and I was just wondering what to do. There is no one here to watch things while I go out. Would you mind watching the house for a bit?" The master of the house went off to call some people.

It was a burden, but since he had no choice, the traveler went over by the hearth and had a smoke. The dead person was an old woman, and she was laid out in an adjoining room. Suddenly, he saw her slowly rise up into a sitting position in bed. He was panic-stricken but controlled himself while looking around quietly. He saw something like a fox in the water drain hole in the kitchen wall. The fox, with its head stuck into the hole, was gazing fixedly at the dead person. Thinking he would take care of that, the man crept quietly out of the house and went around to the back entrance. It was actually a fox standing up on its hind legs with its head stuck into the hole in the wall. He picked up a stick and beat it to death.

—⚉—

102. The evening of the fifteenth day of the New Year is called ko-shogatsu (little New Year). Early in the evening, four or five children form into a group that is called the God (kami) of Fortune. They then go off to visit homes with a bag in hand. As is the custom, they chant "The kami of Fortune are visiting from the Land of the Dawn," and they get rice cakes. Once early evening is past, people never go out on this night. Tradition has it that after midnight on koshogatsu the mountain kami come out and play.

There is a woman called Omasa in Marukodachi in Yamaguchi. She is now about thirty-five or thirty-six years old. Once when she was twelve or thirteen years old, no one is quite sure why, she went out as the kami of Fortune and walked around until late at night. When she was coming home on a lonely road, she met a tall man coming from the opposite direction. His face was bright red and his eyes glared. She threw away her bag and ran home. It is said that she became seriously ill.

—ⁿ—

103. It is said that on the night of *koshogatsu*, or on any winter night with a full moon, the snow woman comes out to play. It is said that she comes bringing children. In the winter, the village children go off to the neighboring hills and have so much fun sleighing that it gets dark before they realize it. They are always warned that on the night of the fifteenth day the snow woman comes out and that they should get home early. Not many people say that they have seen the snow woman.

—ⁿ—

104. There are many rites and ceremonies on the night of *koshogatsu*. *Tsuki-mi*, or the viewing of the months, involves breaking the meat of six walnuts into twelve pieces. The nuts are placed into the fire in the hearth all at the same time, and they are removed all at the same time. The pieces are lined up and counted from the right, as January, February, and so on. If the night of the full moon for a certain month is to be clear, the walnut piece remains burning red. If this night for some month is going to be cloudy, the walnut immediately becomes black. If a month is going to be windy, the walnut piece makes a noise and starts to burn. No matter how many times this is repeated, it always turns out the same. What's uncanny is that the results are the same at every house in the village. The next day, the villagers meet and discuss the results. If, for example, it is said that it will be windy on the night of the full moon of August, they will hurry to harvest the rice that year.[1]

1. Each area has a different form of divination involving grains and monthly cycles. The divination is probably related to the Chinese fortune-telling.

—ⁿ—

105. There is also the practice of *yonaka-mi*, or predicting the year's harvest, which is carried out on the night of *koshogatsu*. Rice cakes are made using different kinds of rice. The rice is shaped into fairly large round cakes. Then the rice grains for each kind of rice

are sprinkled separately on a serving tray. The rice cakes made from the corresponding kinds of rice are placed on top of the grains. These are then covered with a lid until the next morning, when they are examined. It is said that the rice cake that has the most grain stuck to it will yield the best crop for the year. The kinds of rice that should be planted first, in midseason, or later in the planting season are also decided in this way.

—⁓—

106. In Yamada, on the coast, a wonderful scene appears every year. It is said that it is usually the image of a foreign country. It is like some unknown capital with many carriages in the streets and people coming and going. It's quite amazing. It is said that, from year to year, the shapes of the houses and other things do not change in the least.

—⁓—

107. In Kamigo village there is a house called the house on the river, which is on the bank of the Hayase River. One day, a young

Straw Figures for the Rain and Wind Festival

girl in this house went to the edge of the river and picked up some pebbles. A man she had never seen before came up and gave her some tree leaves and things. He was tall and had a red complexion. From this day on, the girl had the power of divination.

This man (*ijin*) was a mountain *kami*, and it is said that the girl became a child of the mountain *kami*.

—⚬—

108. In various places there are people who are said to be possessed by mountain *kami* and can perform divination. There is someone like this in Tsukumoushi village, and his occupation is sawing wood. Magotaro in Kashiwazaki is also possessed. At first, he became mad and seemed in a trance. One day, he went into the mountains and learned the arts and skills of divination from a mountain *kami*. After that it was fantastic how he could read people's innermost thoughts. His methods of divination were completely different from those of the average person. He did not consult any books. He just chatted about everyday things with the person who had come for advice. Then suddenly, in the middle of the discussion, he would stand up and walk to and fro in the family room. Without looking at the person's face, he just said the words that came to mind.

He never failed to be correct. For example, he would say, "Pull up the planks in your wooden-floored room, and then dig up the earth. There should be an old mirror or a piece of a sword there. If you don't remove them in the near future, someone in your family will die or your house will burn down." Then the person would return home, dig, and sure enough the object would be there. There are more examples of this than can be counted on both hands.

—⚬—

109. Around the time of the Bon Festival the villagers make straw figures larger than a person. They are for the Rain and Wind Festival. They carry these figures in a procession to a fork in the road, where they are stood up. They draw the face on paper and use melons to make the male and female body parts. The straw figures used

in the Festival for Warding Off Harmful Insects do not have these body parts and are smaller.

On the occasion of the Rain and Wind Festival the *toya*, or the household in charge of *kami* festivities, is chosen from within the village. After the villagers gather together and drink rice wine, they take the straw figures to the crossroads while playing flutes and beating drums. One kind of flute made from paulownia wood is shaped like a large shell. This is blown loudly.

On this occasion they recite, "We are worshiping the rain and wind of the 210th day (the stormiest day of the year). Which direction shall we worship? Worship toward the north!"[1]

1. According to the *Tong-kuk-yŏ-ji-sung-ram* (*Records of the Land of the Eastern Country*), a fifty-five-volume work on Korean cultural history, in Korea the altar for evil spirits is always built in the northern part of a castle. This practice probably comes from a belief in the *kami* of the north.

—m—

110. Gonge-sama[1] is a large carved wooden figure resembling a lion's head. Each theater troupe that performs *kagura*, a sacred Shinto dance, has one of these heads. Having a head brings divine favor. The Gonge-sama, belonging to the troupe from the Hachiman Shrine in Niibari, met and had a contest with the Gonge-sama of the troupe from Itsukaichi in Tsuchibuchi village. The Gonge-sama from Niibari was defeated and lost one of its ears. Even now it does not have one ear. Each year when the troupe goes around dancing at the villages everyone notices this. The Gonge-sama's special power is in preventing and extinguishing fires.

The troupe mentioned above from Hachiman Shrine once went to Tsukumoushi village. It was getting dark, and they could not find any lodging. They were finally invited to stay at the home of a very poor person. They turned over a nine-liter grain measure and sat the Gonge-sama on top of it. Everyone went to sleep. During the night they were awakened by the noise of something being chewed. They looked and saw that the edge of the eaves had caught on fire. Gonge-sama, atop the grain measure, was leaping up time after time chewing up the flames.

THE LEGENDS OF TONO

If a child has a headache, a request can be made of Gonge-sama to gnaw away the sickness.

1. In Tono *Gongen-sama* is pronounced *Gonge-sama*.

—⚭—

111. In Yamaguchi, Iide, at Tozenji Temple of Arakawa or Hiwatari in Tsukumoushi, at Nakasawa in Aozasa, and Tsuchibuchi in Tsuchibuchi village—in each of these places there is a place named Dan-no-hana.[1] Just off to the side near this place there is always a location called Rendai-no (lotus-platform field). In olden times, it was the custom to send all old people over sixty years of age to the Rendai-no grave site to die. But the old people did not want to die useless, so during the daytime they would come down to the village to work in the fields. In this way, they managed to get enough food to stay alive. This may be the reason that even now, in the area of Yamaguchi in Tsuchibuchi, they say *haka-dachi* (leaving the graves) for going into the fields in the morning, and *haka-agari* (going to the graves) for returning from the fields in the evening.

1. Dan-no-hana indicates the spot where a mound is constructed on a hill. It is believed that the mound was for the worship of the *kami* of the border. Rendai-no was of a similar nature.

—⚭—

112. Dan-no-hana was at one time a fortress where criminals were executed. The lay of the land is for the most part the same as it is in Yamaguchi and Iide of Tsuchibuchi. Dan-no-hana is on a hill at the edge of the village. They have the same place name in Sendai City. Dan-no-hana in Yamaguchi is on the way to Ohora. It is on a hill just past the fortress remains.

Rendai-no is separated off from Dan-no-hana and the houses in Yamaguchi. Marshes surround Rendai-no on all sides. To the east there is a low spot between Rendai-no and Dan-no-hana, and to the south there is a place called Hoshi-ya (star valley).[1] In this area, there are many four-sided sunken spots called *Ezo-yashiki* (Ainu dwellings). These historical sites are quite distinct, and lots of stone tools have been unearthed there. There are two locations in Yamaguchi where Jomon Era stone tools and clay pots have been found. One other location is called Horyo, and the style of pottery found there is quite different from the pottery found in Rendai-no. The objects from Rendai-no do not reflect a superior technique, but the patterns on the objects from Horyo are more advanced. *Haniwa* (terracotta clay figures found in burial mounds) and a variety of stone axes and knives have also been found there. A number of pieces of money called *Ezo-sen* (Ainu coins), which are pottery and about six centimeters in size, have been found in Rendai-no. These coins have a simple swirl-like pattern on them. In Horyo, small beads and tube-shaped objects have also been found. The stone tools found were well crafted and all made from the same kind of stone, even though there are a variety of stones in Rendai-no. In Horyo there are no historical sites, and the area is only about ten thousand meters square. The low spot in Hoshi-ya is now rice fields. The Ainu dwellings are said to have been on both sides of Hoshi-ya. There are two locations in the area where it is said that anyone who digs there will be cursed.

1. Hoshi-ya is the place where the stars are worshiped.

—⚅—

113. In Wano there is a place called Jozuka woods.[1] An elephant is said to be buried there. It is said that this is the only place where there are no earthquakes. Over the years, it has been said that "If there is an earthquake run to Jozuka Woods." This spot must surely be the grave of someone. There is a ditch around the mound. There is a rock on top of the mound. It is said that if anyone digs here they will be cursed.

1. The term *Jozuka* indicates the location for worshiping the *kami* of the border and is probably related to stories from India. One such story is about the demon in hell who is responsible for removing the clothes of souls as they cross over a river.

—⚅—

114. Dan-no-hana in Yamaguchi is now a community graveyard. *Utsugi* bushes are planted around the top of the hill, and the entrance facing to the east looks like a gate. In the center of the gate there is a large moss-covered stone. One time, someone dug under the stone but did not find anything. Later, someone else gave it try and found a large urn. But having been severely scolded by the elders in the village, he put the urn back. It is said that this was prob-

ably the grave of the lord of a fortress. There is a nearby fortress called Bonshasa. Water for the three or four moats surrounding it was obtained by digging canals into the surrounding mountains. There are place names like Tera-yashiki (temple dwelling) and Toi-shi-mori (whetstone woods). A stone wall still standing is said to be the remains of a well. It is said that the ancestors of Magozaemon Yamaguchi lived here. The details of this are recorded in *The Tono Kojiki* (*The Old Records of Tono*, 1763).[1]

1. This is a three-volume work on Tono history, customs, and religion.

—⚭—

115. Fairy tales (*otogibanashi*) start out with the words *mukashi, mukashi*, or "once upon a time." *Yama-haha* (mountain mother) fairy tales are the most numerous. *Yama-haha* probably refers to *Yama-uba* (women living in the mountains who are thought to be she-demons). The following two stories are like this.

—⚭—

116. Once upon a time there were a man and his wife. They had one daughter. One day they had to leave the daughter alone and go into town. They warned her that no matter who came to the house, she should not open the door. They locked the door and left. Frightened, the daughter crouched down by the hearth all alone. Around midday, someone knocked at the door and said, "Open up!" The person yelled, "If you don't open the door I'll kick it down." The girl had no choice but to open the door. In came *Yama-haha* (mountain mother). *Yama-haha* stood astride the master's seat by the hearth and warmed herself by the fire. She ordered, "Cook some food, so I can eat!" The girl obeyed and put out a serving tray with some food on it. While *Yama-haha* was eating, the girl ran away from the house. After she finished eating, *Yama-haha* started chasing the girl. Little by little the distance between them lessened, and just as *Yama-haha* was ready to grab the daughter by the back, they came upon an old man cutting firewood in the hills.

The girl pleaded, "I'm being chased by *Yama-haha*. Please hide me!" Then she hid in the piled up firewood. *Yama-haha* came up and said, "Where is she hiding?" *Yama-haha* started removing the bundles of wood but slipped down the hill holding the wood. The girl took this opportunity to escape. Then she came across an old man cutting reeds. "I'm being chased by *Yama-haha*. Please hide me," she pleaded and hid among the cut reeds. *Yama-haha* came again saying, "Where is she hiding?" She began to remove the bundles of reeds and again slipped down the hill holding on to the reeds. The girl took this chance and ran off again and came to the edge of a large pond. There was nowhere to go from here, so the girl climbed to the top of a large tree beside the pond. *Yama-haha* said, "No matter where you go I will follow you." Then she saw the figure of the girl reflected in the water and jumped right into the pond.

The girl ran off again and came upon a bamboo-leaf hut. She rushed inside and found a young girl there. She repeated her story and then hid in a stone chest. *Yama-haha* came charging in and asked if the girl was there. The young girl said she didn't know anything about it. "No, she must be here," said *Yama-haha*. "I can smell something human." The young girl said, "It may be because I have just roasted a sparrow and eaten it." *Yama-haha* was convinced and said she would sleep for a while. She said, "Shall I sleep in the stone chest—or would the wooden chest be better? The stone one seems cold, so I'll sleep in the wooden one." Then she got into the wooden chest and went to sleep.

The girl from the hut locked the chest, got the other girl out of the stone chest, and said, "I, too, was brought here by *Yama-haha*. Let's kill her and go back to our villages." The girls got an awl, heated it red hot, and made holes in the wooden chest. *Yama-haha* didn't know what was happening and merely said, "Must be field mice." Then the girls boiled some water and poured it into the holes that they had made. They killed *Yama-haha* and returned to their respective homes.

These folktales always close with the saying *kore de dondo hare*, meaning "That's all there is. The end!"

—⚬—

117. Once upon a time there were a man and his wife. They were starting out for town to do some shopping for their daughter's wed-

ding. They locked the door and told their daughter, "Don't open the door even if someone comes." The daughter said "Yes," and they left. Around noon *Yama-haha* came, grabbed the girl, and ate her. She put on the girl's skin and became the girl. In the evening when the parents returned, they called out the girl's name from the gate. "Oriko-himeko, are you there?" "Yes, I am. That was quick," was the reply.

The parents showed her all of the things they had purchased and watched their daughter's happy face. The next day at dawn, their rooster fluttered its wings and crowed, "Look in the corner of the storeroom! Cock-a-doodle-do." The parents thought that this was a rather unusual way for the rooster to crow.

Then the time came to send the bride off. They put who they thought was Oriko-himeko on the horse, and just as they were about to lead her off, the rooster crowed again. They heard it say, "You didn't put Oriko-himeko on the horse. You put *Yama-haha* on it. Cock-a-doo-dle-do." The rooster repeated this, and, for the first time, the parents noticed that something was wrong. They pulled *Yama-haha* down from the horse and killed her. Then they went to look in the corner of the storeroom. There they found many of the girl's bones.

—⚉—

118. In Tono there is also the tale of the two stepsisters Benizara and Kakezara. Kakezara was called Nukabo (tube reed), suggesting something with a hollow center. She was hated by her stepmother but had the blessings of the *kami*. There is a tale of how she eventually became the wife of a *choja*. There are many beautiful scenes in the episode. If I have time some day, I will record all the details.

—⚉—

119. For a long time in the Tono district there has been a song that accompanies the Dance of the Deer.[1] There are slight variations in the song depending upon the village, but I have written below what I heard. This version can be found in a document over a hundred years old.

1. The Dance of the Deer was introduced into the Tono area between the tenth and fifteenth centuries. In the song below, the deer (a deity) visits the world of the town people and shares in their blessings.

SONG FOR THE DANCE OF THE DEER

Blessing the Bridge

Come, look at the bridge!
What important person first crossed it?
Cross this way and that.
Look at the horse-riding area!
We can see to the Great Gate of Sugihara.

Blessing the Gate

Come, look at the gate!
The gate is made of *hinoki* and *sawara* wood.
This is an auspicious silver gate.
Push open the gate doors and look!
Oh, what a wonderful new era!
Come see the Main Hall of the Buddhist Temple!
What carpenter built it?
Long ago a skilled carpenter built it.
He built it with his own hands!

The Song of Kojima

The gate in Kojima is made of *hinoki* and *sawara* wood.
It is an auspicious silver gate.
Push open the doors of the silver gate and look!
Oh, what a wonderful new era!
Yatsumune-style roofs are made of *hinoki* bark.
Karamatsu pines grow even higher.
Springs flow to the left and to the right of the pines.
Scooped and drunk, the water never diminishes.
Morning and evening sun shines on the Great Temple.
A hundred rosy-cheeked children are there.
Auspicious water from heaven for the ink stone.
Standing and waiting for it!

Blessing the Stable

Come, look at the kitchen!
Small and large, sixteen iron pots!
When we cook with sixteen iron pots,
We cut the morning grass with forty-eight horses.
With the horses, we cut *kaya* thatch and *kikyo* flowers with the
morning grass.
The stable is bright with flowers!
The bay horse amid the brightness
Paws the ground with its hoof hoping for a wonderful new era.

When we hear a good singer in this garden,
We are ashamed to dance and sing.
We learned only yesterday what we perform today.
Excuse our mistakes!
It is impossible to say we are good!
Forgive us, let us bow and be on our way.

Blessing the Square

Come, look at this castle!
This garden with four corners and four sides shaped like a
grain measure.
Come, look at this house!
It's the home of a kindhearted person.

Blessing the Town

Come, look at this town!
It is sixty by twenty-eight kilometers.
It is really bustling!

Blessing the Tax Inspector

Come, look at the tax inspector!
He flies his flag in the town.

His houses are in Tachi-machi and Abura-machi.
The inspector rests in the afternoon on the second floor,
    With coins in his pillow and money in his hands.
Come, see this handbill,
    Which we can't obtain or even touch.
A high spot is called "a castle,"
    A low place is called "below the castle."

Blessing the Bridge

Come, and look at the bridge,
    A silver bridge over a golden crossroad.

Blessing a Sacred Place

Come, look at this Buddhist temple!
    Four directions, four sides, all secured with one wedge.
With a fan and prayer beads,
    Going to the temple something good might happen.

Blessing the House

Water on a gold rafter atop a fine column,
    And the roof is so fine as to protect against fire.

The Last Party of the Year

Hearing a good singer in this garden,
    I'm ashamed to sing.
The fine designs on the edge of the flowered straw mats in the
garden.
    The splendid wine cup on a gold and silver lacquered tray,
    Let's move it to the garden.
The seventeen-year-old girl pours wine from a jug.
    The garden brightens with joy.

Drink a cup of this wine,
   And you will live long and prosper.
With the wine goes sea-bream and sea-bass fish,
   And the famous *karu-ume* [plums] of China.
To say we are good is impossible!
   Forgive us, let us bow and be going.

Dance in Front of the Pillar

Between the songs, someone fills in!
   Or the garden will lose its joy.
As soon as it is born, the fawn runs about the hills.
   We, too, go around and run about the garden.
If we place another pillar in the garden,
   The old stag will rub his antlers on it and become young.
Try to grow the pines of Matsushima,   •
   And the stupid ivy clings to it.
The leaves of the ivy, clinging to the Matsushima pines,
   Without good fortune will separate away.
The painted Chinese screens costing nine *kan* in the capital
   Are placed around three and four deep.

Selecting the Deer's Mate

Between the songs, someone fill in!
   Or the garden will lose its joy.
As soon as it is born, the fawn runs about the hills.
   We, too, go around and run about the garden.
Try and go to visit a doe,
   But the mist hangs over Mt. Hakusan.
How happy! The wind removed the mist!
   Off in search of the doe.
No matter how the doe hides,
   I'll search through all the village pampas grass.
Like the leaves of bamboo grass, the pretty doe,
   No matter how she hides, she will be found.

Look at the appearance of the doe and stag;
    Their hearts filled with joy and tenderness.
Deep in the mountains the stag dances,
    For the first time this year.
Burning with passion for a doe,
    The stupid deer can't settle down.
Try to grow the pines of Matsushima,
    And the stupid ivy clings to it.
The leaves of the ivy clinging to the Matsushima pines,
    Without good fortune will separate away,
Out at sea, the plover bird sways with the waves
    And gently flies off.

Offerings of Wine and Money

Who will come to hear this easygoing song?
    Anyone is welcome!
What carpenter made this stand?
    It's square and a treasure plays inside.
What kind of wine do you think this is?
    It's *Kiku-no-sake* from the famous Kaga.
What kind of money do you think this is?
    It's blessed money from a pilgrimage to Ise Shrine or Kumano
Shrine.
Where does this fine paper come from?
    From Harima? From Kashima?
    It folds well and is quality paper.
What is the important part of a fan?
    It's the *uchi-no-miya*, the pivot point.
    The fan folds well and is neat.

TOPICAL
INDEX

GUIDE TO ENGLISH-LANGUAGE WRITINGS ON KUNIO YANAGITA AND *THE LEGENDS OF TONO*

There is a rich and growing literature in Japanese and English about Kunio Yanagita and his many works. The following references are English-language sources available on Yanagita and serve as a guide for further study.

Bernier, Bernard. "Yanagita Kunio's *About Our Ancestors*: Is It a Model for an Indigenous Social Science?" In J. Victor Koschmann, Keibo Oiwa, and Shinji Yamashita, eds., *International Perspectives on Yanagita Kunio and Japanese Folklore Studies*. Ithaca, N.Y.: China-Japan Program, Cornell University, 1985, 65–95.

Christy, Alan S. *Representing the Rural: Place as Method in the Formation of Japanese Native Ethnology, 1910–1945*. Dissertation, University of Chicago, 1997.

Eubanks, Charlotte. "On the Wings of a Bird: Folklore, Nativism, and Meiji Letters," *Asian Folklore Studies* 65, 2006. (This essay looks at Yanagita's work in relation to the writings of *Grimms' Fairy Tales*.)

Figal, Gerald. *Civilization and Monsters: Spirits of Modernity in Meiji Japan*. Durham, N.C./London: Duke University Press, 1999.

Harootunian, H. D. *Things Seen and Unseen: Discourse and Ideology in Tokugawa Nativism*. Chicago: University of Chicago Press, 1988.

———. "Figuring the Folk: History, Poetics, and Representation." In Stephen Vlastos, ed., *Mirror of Modernity: Invented Traditions of Modern Japan*. Berkeley: University of California Press, 1998, 144–59.

———. *Overcome by Modernity: History, Culture and Community in Interwar Japan*. Princeton, N.J.: Princeton University Press, 2000.

———. "Disciplinizing Native Knowledge and Producing Place: Yanagita Kunio, Origuchi Shinobu, Takata Yasuma." In J. T. Rimer, ed., *Culture and Identity: Japanese Intellectuals during the Interwar Years*. Princeton, N.J.: Princeton Uniersity Press, 1990, 99–127.

Hashimoto, Mitsuru. "Chiho: Yanagita Kunio's Japan." In Stephen Vlastos, ed., *Mirror of Modernity: Invented Traditions of Modern Japan*. Berkeley: University of California Press, 1998, 133–44.

Inoue, Hisashi. *Shinshaku Tōno monogatari (A New Reading of the Tales of Tōno)*. Tokyo: Chikuma shobo, 1976. (This is a collection of nine stories by the novelist Inoue that play off of Yanagita's original Tono work. A translation of this work has been completed by Christopher Robins.)

Inouye, Charles. *The Similitude of Blossoms: A Critical Biography of Izumi Kyoka (1873-1939), Japanese Novelist and Playwright*. Cambridge, Mass.: Harvard University Press, 1998.

Ishida, Eiichiro. "Unfinished but Enduring: Yanagita Kunio's Folklore Studies," *Japan Quarterly* 10, no. 1 (January–March 1963): 35–42.

Ishii, Yoko. *Kunio Yanagita: The Life and Times of a Japanese Folklorist*. Master's thesis. University of Calgary, 1998. See http://dspace.ucalgary.ca/handle/1880/26004.

Ivy, Marilyn. *Discourses of the Vanishing: Modernity, Phantasm, Japan*. Chicago: University of Chicago Press, 1995.

Kawada, Minoru. *The Origin of Ethnography in Japan: Yanagita Kunio and His Times*. London: Kegan Paul International, 1993. (See Ronald Morse's review of this book in *Monumenta Nipponica* 56, no. 3, [Autumn 1995].)

Koschmann, J. Victor. "Folklore Studies and the Conservative Anti-establishment in Modern Japan." In J. Victor Koschmann, Keibo Oiwa, and Shinji Yamashita, eds., *International Perspectives on Yanagita Kunio and Japanese Folklore Studies*. Ithaca, N.Y.: China-Japan Program, Cornell University, 1985, 131–64.

Lummis, Douglas C. "Yanagita Kunio's Critique of the Chrysanthemum and the Sword: An Annotated Translation." *Tsudajuku Daigaku, Kokusai Kankei Kenkyu*, no. 24, (March 1998): 125–40.

Makita, Shigeru. "World Authority on folklore: Yanagita Kunio." *Japan Quarterly* (Tokyo) 20, no. 3 (July–September 1973): 283–93.

Mayer, Fanny Hagin, tr. and ed. *The Yanagita Kunio Guide to the Japanese*

Folk Tale. Bloomington: Indiana University Press, 1986.

———. "The Yanagita Kunio Approach to Japanese Folklore Studies." *The Transactions of the Asiatic Society of Japan,* third series 13 (1976): 129–43.

———. "Available Japanese Folk Tales." *Monumenta Nipponica* 24, no. 3 (1969): 235–47.

———. "Japanese Folk Humor." *Asian Folklore Studies* 41–2 (1982): 187–99.

Mishima, Yukio. "Two Essays by Mishima Yukio on Yanagita Kunio." *DELOS* 1, no. 3 (1988): 119–25. (These essays translated by J. Thomas Rimer are Mishima's 1970 and 1972 reflections on *The Legends of Tono.*)

Miwa, Kimitada. "Toward a Rediscovery of Localism: Can the Yanagita School of Folklore Studies Overcome Japan's Modern Ills?" *Japan Quarterly* (Tokyo) 23, no. 1 (January–March 1976): 44–52.

Mori, Koichi. "Yanagita Kunio: An Interpretative Study." *Japanese Journal of Religious Studies* (Tokyo) 7, nos. 2–3 (June–September 1980): 83–115.

Morse, Ronald A. "Personalities and Issues in Yanagita Kunio Studies." *Japan Quarterly* (Tokyo) 22, no. 3 (July–September 1975): 239–54.

———. *Yanagita Kunio and the Folklore Movement: The Search for Japan's National Character and Distinctiveness.* New York: Garland, 1990 (Garland Folklore Library, 2).

———. "Tono Monogatari Ko" (Thoughts on *Tono monogatari*). *Tenbo,* no. 207 (March 1976): 71–80.

———. "Yanagita Kunio, and The Modern Japanese Consciousness." In J. Victor Koschmann, Keibo Oiwa, and Shinji Yamashita, eds., *International Perspectives on Yanagita Kunio and Japanese Folklore Studies.* Ithaca, N.Y.: China-Japan Program, Cornell University, 1985, 11–28.

———. "An Introduction to The Legends of Tono and Yanagita Kunio." *DELOS* 1, no. 3 (1988): 95–125.

Oiwa, Keibo. "An Approach to Yanagita Kunio's View of Language." In J. Victor Koschmann, Keibo Oiwa, and Shinji Yamashita, eds., *International Perspectives on Yanagita Kunio and Japanese Folklore Studies.* Ithaca, N.Y.: China-Japan Program, Cornell University, 1985, 121–30.

Olson, Lawrence. *Ambivalent Moderns: Portraits of Japanese Cultural Identity.* Lanham, Md.: Rowman & Littlefield Publishers, Inc., 1992.

Ortabasi, Melek. *Japanese Cultural History as Literary Landscape: Scholarship, Authorship and Language in Yanagita Kunio's Native Ethnology.* Dissertation, University of Washington, 2001.

Rimer, Thomas J., trans. "Two Essays by Mishima Yukio on Yanagida

Kunio." *DELOS* 1, no. 3 (1988): 119–25. (These essays are Mishima's thoughts on *Tono monogatari.*)

Sadler, A. W. "The Spirit-Captives of Japan's North Country: Nineteenth Century Narratives of the Kamikakushi." *Asian Folklore Studies* 46, no. 2 (1987): 217–26.

Sakamoto, Kiyo. "Tono Monogatari as Performance: Literary Representation of the Legends of Tono by Yanagita Kunio." In Eiji Sekine, ed., *Japanese Theatricality and Performance.* West Lafayette, Ind.: Midwest Association for Japanese Literary Studies, 1995 (Proceedings of the Midwest Association for Japanese Studies, vol. 1), 172–88.

Sato, Kenji. "The Research of Yanagita Kunio: The 1960s and Today." *Social Science Japan,* no. 15 (March 1999): 20–21.

Tada, Michitaro. "Japanese Sensibility: An Imitation of Yanagita." In J. Victor Koschmann, Keibo Oiwa, and Shinji Yamashita, eds., *International Perspectives on Yanagita Kunio and Japanese Folklore Studies.* Ithaca, N.Y.: China-Japan Program, Cornell University, 1985, 97–120.

Takayanagi, Shun'ichi. "In Search of Yanagita Kunio: A Review Article on the Legends of Tono by Kunio Yanagita." *Monumenta Nipponica* (Tokyo) 31, no. 2 (Summer 1976): 165–78 (Review of Morse's translation of *The Legends of Tono*).

Tayama, Katai. *Literary Life in Tokyo 1885–1915.* Translated by Kenneth G. Henshall. Leiden: E. J. Brill, 1987.

Toda, Shizuo. *Tono monogatari: Folklore and Tradition in the Tono Districts.* Sendai, September 1983. The work was printed in Sendai City but is not for sale. (This translation of *Tono monogatari* includes 299 tales from the 1935 expanded edition of the work. The translator's introduction and comments are in Japanese. The translation does not include legends 11, 43, 68, 85, 112, 118, and 119 or the song from the end of the original 1910 version.)

Tsurumi, Kazuko. *The Collected Works of Kazuko Tsurumi: Tsurumi Kazuko Mandara* (in Japanese), eleven volumes. Fujiwara Shoten, 1999. (Volume 10, "Creativity in Social Science: A Theory of Endogenous Development," contains ten essays in English related to Yanagita Kunio. Volume 11 is also English-language essays. Tsurumi's Japanese-language essays on Yanagita Kunio can be found in volume 4 of this same collection.)

Vlastos, Stephen, ed. *Mirror of Modernity: Invented Traditions of Modern Japan.* Berkeley: University of California Press, 1998.

Yamashita, Shinji. "Ritual and 'Unconscious Tradition': A Note on Yanagita Kunio's *About Our Ancestors.*" In J. Victor Koschmann, Keibo Oiwa, and

Shinji Yamashita, eds., *International Perspectives on Yanagita Kunio and Japanese Folklore Studies*. Ithaca, N.Y.: China-Japan Program, Cornell University, 1985, 55–64.

Yanagita, Kunio. *About Our Ancestors: The Japanese Family System*. Trans. Fanny Hagin Mayer and Ishiwara Yasuyo. New York: Greenwood, 1988.

———. *Japanese Folk Tales: A Revised Selection*. Translation by Fanny Hagin Mayer; illustrated by Kei Wakana. Tokyo News Service, Ltd., 1968

———. "Opportunities for Folklore Research in Japan." In Richard M. Dorson, ed., *Studies in Japanese Folklore*. Bloomington: Indiana University Press, 1963.

———. *The Legends of Tono*. Trans. Ronald A. Morse. Tokyo: Japan Foundation 1975. (Contains the introduction by folklore expert, Richard M. Dorson, reproduced in this edition).

———. "The Evolution of Japanese Festivals: From Matsuri to Sairei." Translated with an introduction by Stephen Nussbaum. In J. Victor Koschmann, Keibo Oiwa, and Shinji Yamashita, eds., *International Perspectives on Yanagita Kunio and Japanese Folklore Studies*. Ithaca, N.Y.: China-Japan Program, Cornell University, 1985, 167–202.

ABOUT
THE TRANSLATOR

Ronald A. Morse lives in Las Vegas, Nevada, with his wife Jacqueline. He was the Tokyo Foundation Professor of Japan Studies at the University of Nevada in 2004 and 2005 and the Paul I. Terasaki Professor of Japanese Studies at the University of California, Los Angeles (UCLA), from 2001 to 2004. From 1996 to 2001, he was professor of economics and business administration at Reitaku University in Tokyo, Japan.

Dr. Morse finished his translation of *The Legends of Tono* in 1975 after he completed his doctoral thesis at Princeton University on Kunio Yanagita and the Japanese folklore movement. He spent the next two decades working for the U.S. government at the Defense, State, and Energy Departments in Washington, D.C.

From 1981 to 1988, he was the director of the Asia Program at the Woodrow Wilson International Center for Scholars, a presidential memorial in Washington, D.C., and then served as a special assistant for policy to the Librarian of Congress (1989–1990). From 1990 to 1991, he helped establish and was executive vice president of the Economic Strategy Institute, a Washington, D.C., think tank focused on global business competition.

Over the years Morse has established himself as a prominent commentator on U.S-Asian affairs. He is the author of twenty-one books on Asian issues and was contributor to numerous journals and newspapers. He earned his B.A. in Chinese studies from the University of California, Berkeley. His son, Randall Alexander Morse, lives in Annapolis, Maryland.